# SILENT HARMONY

# SILENT HARMONY

## FAIRMONT RIDING ACADEMY:

*A Vivienne Taylor Horse Lover's Mystery*

• BOOK 1 •

**SKYSCAPE**

# SILENT HARMONY

## SKYSCAPE

The characters and events portrayed in this book are fictitious. Any similarity to
real persons, living or dead, is coincidental and not intended by the author.

Text copyright © 2013 Michele Scott

Amazon Publishing
Attn: Amazon Children's Publishing
P.O. Box 400818
Las Vegas, NV 89140
www.amazon.com/amazonchildrenspublishing

Library of Congress Cataloging-in-Publication Data is available upon request.

ISBN-13: 9781477817131 (paperback)
ISBN-10: 1477817131 (paperback)
ISBN-13: 9781477867136 (eBook)
ISBN-10: B00BHIFQ3K (eBook)

Editor: Tim Ditlow

Printed in The United States of America (R)
First edition
10 9 8 7 6 5 4 3 2 1

*To my daughter Kaitlin.*
*You are a blessing, and watching you ride your*
*Mr. Monty brings me more joy than you'll ever know.*
*You two were a huge inspiration for this series.*
*I love you.*

CHAPTER *one*

I don't like being afraid.

And if I look at it logically, I really shouldn't be *this* scared. Except that I *am* moving fifteen hundred miles away from my family, my friends, and my horses. And, reminder to self—it's all for a chance to achieve every goal and dream I've ever had.

That being the case, you'd think I'd be a little more excited and a little less totally messed up in the brain—like a swirly-twirl-of-colors-blending-until-I-get-dizzy kind of messed up. The kind of messed up that makes you feel like you want to puke. My mom says it's "just nerves" and that it's normal for me to feel this way. But, here's the thing: my mom and I both know that I am *so not normal*. And if the kids at my new school—excuse me, at the *Academy*—find out how not normal I am, well, it likely wouldn't be so good for me.

Here's the thing: I'm not idiotic enough to think that I am going to walk into the Fairmont Riding Academy for Young Equestrians to a chorus of "Welcome, Vivienne Taylor! We are so thrilled that you're here and can't wait to become your lifelong friends." Not by kids with horses that cost more than our house. Kids who drive expensive cars from Germany. Kids who think Target is something they shoot at while out on expensive weekend hunting vacations with their fathers, not a place where people can buy comforter sets that include sheets for under fifty bucks, cool T-shirts, and pretty-smelling candles.

And I have to face facts: I *am* different from them. My mom is a single parent who's worked her butt off as a large-animal vet to support my brother and me and make sure that I've had the best three-day event training that we could possibly get within driving distance of our small Oregon town. She knows just how important my dream is to compete someday in the Olympics. Thus, the working off of her butt.

It's been about a month since I received the letter from the Fairmont Academy letting me know that I had been chosen for their annual scholarship. My first three thoughts: *Me? Me? Me!* The only chance someone like me will ever have to attend Fairmont is through this scholarship.

So I do realize that I *should* be completely excited and way less stressed out about it. But tell that to my brain, and maybe, I have to admit, to my heart.

"Sweetie, wake up. I need your help." It's well past midnight, and Mom's voice is tense as she stands in the doorway of my room. I know immediately what she needs. "I'm sorry about this, Vivvie."

"No worries, Mom. I was awake. Just thinking about stuff." I pick my jeans up off the floor and slip out of my pajama pants and into them. I look around for my Thomas Jefferson High sweatshirt. "Who's gonna stay with Cole?"

"I've put Sadie and Georgia in your brother's room. I wish Grandma were here, but two Rotties might actually be better protection. I'll lock up and meet you in the truck. Thanks, Shnoopy," she says, calling me her favorite pet name, which is somewhat embarrassing when said in front of my friends, but she's my mom and, truth be told, I kinda like the nickname after all these years.

"What do we have?" I ask as I climb into the truck.

"A thirteen-year-old mare down in Albany. Owner went to bring her in from pasture for the night and noticed she was severely bloated and seemed to be having problems breathing."

"Too many causes to choose from." I zip up my sweatshirt and pull my hood on. It seems cold for a late August night, or maybe that's just me. I always tend to be a bit chilly.

Mom glances at me through weary blue eyes as she punches in the address on the GPS. "That's why I'm bringing you."

I nod and reach into the backseat to scavenge for a Diet Pepsi among the vet reports, bandages, books, junk food, dog leashes, and dog toys. Professionally speaking, my mom can detail a report to clients like nobody's business, but she tends to be less focused and orderly when it comes to this truck and our house. *Way* less focused. I try to pick up the slack on these things. "Want one?" I hold up the soda can.

"I was actually up working on some reports and had a couple of cups of coffee to keep me going. I just had a feeling about tonight. Why were *you* still awake?"

I shrug. "Don't know. Just couldn't sleep." *Because I'm secretly scared to death and can't stop obsessing about leaving home.* "What's up with this woman just calling us now if her horse is this sick? I mean, wouldn't she have brought her in from the pasture in the early part of the evening?"

"When I asked her what time she brought her in, she said it was only an hour ago."

"And it's one o'clock in the morning," I say, noticing the clock on the dashboard.

"Something tells me she may have been out on a late night and just forgot about her horse."

"Oh, she's one of *those*."

"Careful, Vivvie."

We pull up to a small, worn-out house with a ramshackle barn in the back. There are three horses in one of the corrals, and a decent-size pasture. Mom pulls up next to the barn. Its dim light casts shadows on the hard-packed ground. I grab a flashlight.

"Hi, Ms. Harris. I'm Dr. Taylor. This is my daughter, Vivienne," my mom says to a skinny, overly bleached blond woman. I take note of a deep sadness in the horse owner's dark eyes, detectable even in this weak lighting.

"Oh, you can call me Rebecca. I got your number from my neighbor, Gary Ferguson, a few miles up the road. He says you're the best. Thank you for coming out so late. You think she's colicking?"

Colic tends to be the initial go-to guess for most backyard horse owners. It's an easy assumption but not always correct. Horses have this delicate digestive tract, and when they get stomachaches, they can't puke. Instead, they roll on the ground, seeking some kind of relief. But the scary thing is that when they roll, their intestines can twist, and that can kill them. Colic surgery is expensive, and if the condition isn't caught early enough, the consequences are deadly.

"Has she been rolling?" Mom asks.

"No. Just been down," the woman says, her voice all shaky and her eyes filling with tears. "You gotta help her."

Mom touches her on the shoulder. "I'll do whatever I can."

The other three horses watch us, all of them sensing something bad. I face them for a few seconds and nod. I close my eyes briefly and take in a deep breath. *My mother is a healer. We are here to help.*

One of the horses—a little paint—bobs his head once and then lowers it to the ground. In the shadow of the light I notice him pawing the ground for several seconds. Then he begins to lick and chew on his mouth, an act of submission. He *understands* me. He knows what I've told him.

I see the mare on the ground, frothing at the mouth. *This isn't good. Rabies?* Her belly is completely distended, and there's a familiar rotten-sweet smell in the stall. *Diarrhea.*

My mother kneels near her head and strokes her face. "It's okay, mare."

"What's her name?" I ask Rebecca.

"Summer."

Mom places her stethoscope over the area of Summer's heart. "Vivvie, come here. See what you get from this."

Mom moves to the mare's rear end to take her temperature. A few seconds later she says, "One hundred and four. Could mean an infection. Or maybe a virus?" Mom sucks in a deep breath and eyeballs me.

*Think.* It's a high temp for an adult horse. They're usually about the same as us—between ninety-eight and ninety-nine degrees.

I quickly kneel down next to Summer, who, though in obvious agony, lifts her head slightly as I place my hand on her face. Her weak groan echoes off the steel walls of the stall. "It's not colic." I glance at my mother.

"Piroplasmosis? Tularemia?" Mom suggests, referring to awful tick-induced diseases. "Her pulse is so thready."

I rub my hands over the horse's entire body, searching for the disgusting parasites. "No. I don't think so. No ticks." Then I slide one hand under Summer's face, and place the other on the opposite side of her cheek. "Hi, sweet girl. Hi. Can you help us help you? I know you hurt. I know."

Everything grows silent and still in the stall. Even the dust particles floating in the haze of the light stop swirling. Summer's eyes are fluttering. Suddenly, I feel a deep shudder travel through her, kicking up a plume of dust underneath her legs.

*Water. Bad.*

"Is she gonna die?" Rebecca squeals. "What's happening?"

My mother quickly kneels down next to me. "It's the pasture," I tell her. "Cowbane—it's in the water."

"Oh my God," Mom says. She turns and looks at Rebecca. "How much grass do you have in your pasture?"

Rebecca twists her hands nervously. "I'm not sure. It's been a bit dry."

Summer is convulsing again. This time as I scan her body, I

notice the deep crevice in her hindquarters. I stand up and shine my flashlight on the other horses. All are severely underweight.

I hear Mom ask, "What about water? Is there water out in the pasture?"

"There's a ditch that fills up when we get showers here. It's just, I haven't had the money to put good seed down for some time."

"And we haven't had a good shower for a couple of weeks," I say. "I'm guessing you haven't provided clean water for these animals all summer." As the heat rises in my cheeks I have to bite my lip not to say more. Same old story, seen way too many times—another client who has no business owning horses.

"Hey, there's enough feed out there. And we, we—we have gotten some rain. Hell, it mists here every morning." Rebecca straightens her shoulders as she says this; her deeply lined face stretches taut.

I stare at this idiot as my mother breezes past me, headed to the truck. "Let's just keep focused, Vivvie," she whispers.

"There's poison in that pasture," I continue. "It's coming from the source you *think* is a decent watering hole. Your horse here is probably going to die because of it. My mom will have to treat all your animals who either drank or ate it. And just so you know, no horse will eat cowbane unless they're starving."

Rebecca's jaw drops. "I didn't know. I really didn't know."

"Oh, I believe you. But you *should* have."

Mom brings back two IV bags and an IV setup.

"Sodium nitrate and thiosulfate?" I ask.

She nods grimly. "Please go to the truck and get me some electrolytes, Banamine, and carbamazepine."

I run to the truck and slide open one of the drawers that holds these meds.

Summer doesn't fight Mom as she gets the IVs started. Next, Mom injects her with Banamine. We have to get her fever down fast. The injection of carbamazepine is to stop the seizures. I stay kneeling at Summer's head, talking to her, stroking the small white star she has on her forehead. "You like green apples best, don't you?" I keep petting her as Mom begins pumping in the other meds. "How about little kids? You like little kids?"

The mare closes her eyes as another shudder racks her body. "I know a little girl who would love to meet you. Her name is Kimmy. I babysit her sometimes. She's seven and very sweet. They have a pony named Ziggy, but they would love a pretty girl like you. Kimmy would feed you green apples every day."

*Tired.*

I feel Summer's body relaxing.

*Sick.*

I sigh. "I know. Don't worry. We won't make you stay here. There *are* greener pastures."

Mom gives me a sharp look and shakes her head.

*Friends.*

I glance at Mom before whispering into Summer's ear. "Your friends? We can help them too. But it's your choice, girl. Your choice. You don't have to stay here."

We pump more meds and electrolytes into her over the next hour. Mom places a call to the emergency hospital and asks for a trailer to be brought out. Summer is shaky on her legs, but we are able to get her loaded onto the trailer when it arrives.

"Who's gonna pay for this?" Rebecca hollers. "I don't have money for a fancy vet hospital. If I knew you was gonna call them, I'd have put her down."

"I'll pay," Mom says. "I will pay her medical bills."

I glance at her with a sharp look. She shrugs.

"Okay," Rebecca replies meekly.

"But understand, this means that Summer is now my horse. And I'm going to treat your other three. And I'm sorry, but they will need to be removed from your property."

"I *never* mistreat my animals," Rebecca sobs.

"Neglect is just as bad."

"But I called you! That's not neglect."

After closing the trailer door and letting the driver know that she'll be at the hospital as soon as she takes care of the other three horses, Mom turns and faces Rebecca full-on. "Rebecca, it's simple, really. Can you properly take care of these animals right here and now?" she asks. "Can you afford them? Is it fair to them to leave them out in a pasture at all hours without any real feed and expose them to contaminated food and water? Do you think it matters to them that you didn't know about it?"

Rebecca stares hard at her. "Guess not," she mutters.

"Okay then. I think we all know what needs to happen."

I help treat the other horses. Each shows symptoms of toxicity. And we still don't know whether any will survive. The next several hours will be crucial.

When we finish up three hours later, Rebecca has gone back into her house. When Mom told her that someone would be out by 9:00 a.m. to pick up the remaining horses, she didn't say one word.

*Yeah, what can you say?* I think.

It is heartbreaking and horrible. And way, way too common.

Back in the truck, Mom glances up at me as she finishes writing down her notes. "I know."

"No, you don't."

"Uh-huh, I sure do," she says.

"Come on, Mom. It's just, I worry about you. How are you supposed to pay for Summer's care at the vet hospital, and who is going to take in those other three horses? Mom?"

She cocks an eyebrow. "I make a decent living."

"That's not—"

"I'll work a few extra hours."

"I know you will! But you need a life. And with me going away, you'll only have Cole."

"And Grandma."

"Fabulous. A seven-year-old and a seventy-year-old. I want you to, I don't know, go out with your friends once in a while. All you do is work."

She takes my hand. "Shnoopy, this *is* my life. You, your brother, and these animals. And once I fatten those four up, by the time you come home at Christmas, I guarantee all four will be with responsible, loving new owners."

I sigh, lean back, close my eyes. I want to argue with her, but here's the thing: I would do the exact same thing. Not the sensible thing, the practical thing, or the easy thing. But for us, it's the only thing.

CHAPTER *two*

s soon as we get home, I grab a cup of coffee, fry up some bacon and eggs for Mom, Cole, and me. I should probably go and get some rest, but the sun is up, and there are a few people that I need to say good-bye to.

"You should lie down for an hour or two, Vivvie," Mom says. "Long night."

Cole looks up at me with his sleepy blue eyes. He takes a bite of the eggs—with extra-extra cheese, just the way he likes them. "You can watch TV with me," he says.

I ruffle the top of his hair. "Not today, C-man. I'm going over to Gail's and say my good-byes. I just got a text from her while I was making the grand slam breakfast, and she says that she has something for me."

Cole frowns and doesn't offer any reply.

"Agreed," Mom says, getting up to rinse her plate. "With your leaving tomorrow, this is probably your only chance to tell the crew good-bye."

"I want you to stay here," Cole whines.

*Okay.* Even though he thinks that what he means is that he just wants me to stay and watch some TV with him, I know that my little brother is really telling me he doesn't want me to leave for Fairmont. "You're gonna have to get used to me not being around, bud."

"I know that." He nods and picks at his food.

"C'mon, some of it'll be good. You won't have me taking up all that time in the bathroom, and you can watch all your stupid shows."

"They're not stupid!" He tosses a napkin at me. "At least I won't have to watch your dumb *lover* shows, where people always make out and stuff. Those are stupid."

I walk back to my room laughing, but inside I know my little brother is feeling . . . a little sad. A little scared. Like me.

And I wonder if my leaving brings up other stuff. Granted, Cole never got to know our so-called dad—Lane Taylor. He was only three months old and I had just turned ten the day before he left us—without any explanation, as far as I know. Just left. I could tell that Mom was confused, hurt, and angry. I was just confused—at first. My dad was the one who had put me on the back of a horse when I was only two. The one who instilled the love of eventing in me. My dad was that dad who came to school functions and pony club meetings. Now, he's just . . . gone.

After a couple of years, I did some investigating. It didn't take me long to find him. My dad is fairly well known in the eventing circles on the East Coast.

Within a year of leaving us, he had a new wife and baby.

Yeah—new baby. I have a little sister out there whom I've never met. And, I still have plenty of questions for Lane. Maybe someday I will get the chance to ask him personally for some answers.

Anyway, a weird upside to my father's abandonment is that my mom, Cole, and I are about as tight as a family can be. Though Cole is often a Giant Pain in the Butt, I love him to pieces and would go to the end of the earth to protect him. Breaking us up to go away to Fairmont? My stomach twists every time I think about it. But on the flip side—the selfish side—I know this is not an opportunity that I can pass up.

Keys in hand, I holler back to Mom, "I'll be home in a bit."

"Drive careful, Shnoopy. I'll be working on reports, unless I get an emergency call."

I bound down the front porch steps and glance out at the pasture where Mom has already turned out the crew. Dean lifts his head and eyes me. "Treats, later, sweetie guy." I'm putting off my good-byes to the horses until the last minute—about twenty-four rapidly approaching hours from now.

Behind the wheel of my old Chevy truck—grayish beige with a light coating of rust—I put my headphones on, turn on the iPod, and find some Miranda Lambert.

Window down and all is right in my world as I head over to see the woman who has been my trainer for the past seven years. Gail only lives ten minutes away, which is good because that means we've always been able to keep Dean at home and just trailer over for lessons. Ever since Mom let me get my license I've been able to trailer him over to Gail's myself. Since I turned thirteen I've worked summers at Gail's in trade for my lessons. I suspect this helped Mom sock away enough cash to surprise me with the truck on my last birthday.

Gail's place is called Hidden Trail Ranch—an eight-stall main barn with in-and-outs, eight corrals with overhangs. She also has a dressage court, a jump arena, and a round pen. It's basically my home away from home, and I love it.

Gail never keeps more than sixteen horses on the property. She runs the local Young Equestrians group. There are twelve of us altogether, including Kate, Mia, and Austen—my best friends.

I pull the truck up in front of the main barn and spot Gail walking her gelding, Jeepers, inside.

"Hey, Vivvie," she says. "Shouldn't you be packing?"

I walk into the breezeway. "Packed!" I smile at her. "Plus, you texted me and said you wanted me to come by."

"That's right. I did want you to stop by. I forgot." She laughs. "I am not as organized or focused as you. That's our V, always prepared and ready to go. Or is it that you just can't wait to get out of here?" She turns to look at me, smiling, her hazel eyes twinkling.

"Are you kidding me? Leaving you guys is the hardest thing I've ever had to do."

Gail wraps her arms around me and pulls me in to her. "You'll be great. I've done all I can, and you know you're ready for some coaches who can help you move up to the next level."

I lower my head. "I'm just not so sure if . . ."

"Stop right there, V. This is the exact right move for you. We both know it. Now, don't get me all upset. I've got a date tonight. Can't be all pink-eyed and puffy-faced."

"Where are you and Jason going?"

"Don't know. It's a surprise."

I don't think Gail has ever been married, and I know she's almost fifty. But we all like Jason, one of our local farriers, a lot. I wonder whether—hope, actually—my mom might find someone, someday soon. But I know how badly Lane crushed her, and I'm not sure she'll ever give another guy a chance.

"Will you go into the house and let Trudy out?" Gail asks. "Old girl needs some exercise. You'll probably have to drag her off her doggie bed. I'll be right in to give you a little gift."

I rub my hands together. "You got it." I head up to the house, which is just back behind the barn and arenas. Opening the front door of the ranch-style house, I take a few steps inside and call out for Trudy, an ancient Jack Russell terrier. The house seems eerily quiet. *Wonder what's—*

"Surprise!" Kate, Mia, Austen, and the rest of the crew scream and scramble out from behind the couch, drapes, doors, even from under tables. Suddenly Gail is behind me, her hands on my shoulders.

"What?" I squeal.

"We couldn't send you off without a party!" Mia says. Kate moves over to the stereo, and one of my favorite songs blares into the room.

I see Austen standing in the background, a smirky smile across his dimpled face. He winks at me. He is wearing what he always wears when he wants to bug Gail and make me laugh.

*Oh, Austen.*

Austen Giles. My first major crush. And a major joker. And the outfit—boots, a T-shirt, and over his riding breeches a pair of boxers with Stewie from *Family Guy* on the, um . . . as Austen refers to it, the bonus area. He turns around and shows me the back view—it says "Boy Toy." I walk over to him, and those irresistible dimples deepen, his blue eyes shine a little brighter. I am so going to miss this guy.

"I've got something for you to remember me by, Vivvie."

"You do?"

He takes off the boxers to a chorus of whistles and giggles. How can I not have a crush on Austen Giles? Good looking, funny, smart, but also my friend for so long that nothing's ever *really* happened between us. And now he's off to UC Davis and I am off to Fairmont. So our little flirtation will be left behind in Albany . . . for now.

He hands me the boxers. "Wear them proudly."

"I doubt that very seriously," I reply and take the boxers from him. "But I will wear them."

The afternoon wears on with more laughs, good food, music, and sharing memories of horse shows, events, and fun times. But now it's getting late, so I hug my friends, fight back the tears. We promise each other that Christmas break will be like none other when we can all be together again.

Gail gives me one last hug and hands me a small green-wrapped box. Green is my color. As an eventer, we tend to pick a favorite color and in some way, shape, or form display it on ourselves or our horses during the cross-country phase. I have a green saddle pad and I wear a green helmet cover over my skullcap. As Mia and Kate stand there wearing goofy grins on their faces, I open up the box, and inside I find a silver charm bracelet with a charm that represents each one of my best friends. "Ice-cream cone for you?" I point to Mia.

She nods, tears in her eyes, and moves in to hug me. "I am so gonna miss you. You have a blast down in Cali. Kick some ass out there for me!"

I nod, speechless. This is so hard. I look back down at the bracelet and laugh when I see the octopus charm. "Kate mate!" We both laugh, remembering how we babysat Cole one night when he was only three, and we could not get him to stop crying for my mom. The only thing that got him to stop was Kate pretending to be an octopus. That's the short version of the story, but trust me, it was hilarious.

Ah, a charm with a pair of boxers. I smile at Austen. "How in the world did you find this?"

"It wasn't easy," he replies, with his signature devilish grin.

Finally, the charm from Gail is of a horse head, its eye is a green emerald. "It's beautiful. Thank you, Gail."

"Read the back," she insists.

I turn the bracelet over and read the inscription: *We love you, V. Team Get 'er Done.* I laugh through my tears. That was us—all of us. When each of us would head out on cross-country during an event, we'd always say in support, "Go get 'er done."

"God, I love you guys."

We have one last group hug, all of us getting a little weepy.

Austen walks me out to my truck. "I want to give you something else," he says as we reach the driver-side door.

"I don't know if I can take any more." I laugh. "What is it?"

"This." He edges me back against the truck and kisses me. A non-buddy kind of kiss.

*Okay . . . I never thought—*

"That's to be sure that you don't forget me."

"I would never—nope." I shake my head, a slow smile spreading across my face. "Right. I'll see you at Christmas." I climb into the truck and hope I can remember how to drive, knowing that I will not be forgetting Austen any time soon.

CHAPTER *three*

It is less than twenty-four hours later and I've officially decided that good-byes suck. I thought yesterday was hard, but it was nothing compared to this morning. I am usually much tougher than this. What's the point in crying? I cried out most of my tears after Lane left us. At least I thought I had, until this morning.

"Oh, Vivvie, don't. Please," Mom says. "You know, my eyes get all puffy and my nose gets all stuffed up and, well, just stop. You *should* be happy." Mom tosses back her long auburn hair, which is a little darker than my own. She pushes mine back behind my shoulders, wipes my face, and tilts her head toward the stall door where Dean, my big bay Thoroughbred gelding, stands. His large brown eyes watch us. "I think someone wants to say good-bye."

I nod but am unable to look at him just yet. "I *am* happy. I mean, it's a once-in-a-lifetime opportunity. I get that. It's just—I'm going to miss you, Dean, sort of Grandma, and even Cole when I don't have someone to hassle. And who is going to clean up after you?

Your truck is worse than the inside of a barn." I muster a semi-fake smile.

"That's my girl. Sarcastic, lovable, and all rolled up into one five-foot-three, talented-and-tough-as-nails young woman."

"Hillarie, it's getting late! We don't want her to miss her flight," my grandmother yells from the front porch. Grandma will have my room redecorated before my flight lands at LAX. A thought that makes me cringe for many reasons. No more posters of my favorite riders—Steffen Peters, McClain Ward, Will Simpson, Karen O'Connor, and Gina Miles. Pretty sure she'll also take down all of the ribbons I've won over the years, which I've strung across the top of the walls.

But what bothers me most is that I know for a fact my grandmother will drive my mom crazy insane. Mom needs her while I'm away, though. With Mom having to make emergency calls in the middle of the night, someone besides our dogs has to be there for my brother. It had been me for the past few years. Grandma is all too eager to take my place. She loves to tell Mom her every thought about what needs to be done around the house, what kind of parent Mom should be, and on and on. Leaving my mom to deal with my grandma put a pang of guilt right in the center of my heart. *Even though it is the best opportunity in the world.*

To be worth all of this, this opportunity had better land me a spot on Fairmont's Young Equestrians team. Young Equestrians prepares hopefuls for the US Equestrian Team, which in turn creates Olympic-caliber riders. I will have my junior year to earn a place on the Fairmont team. After that, I'll need to hold on to that position during my senior year and college career.

The introduction letter I'd received from the academy stated: *We at Fairmont Academy look forward to helping you take the first step in achieving your goal of becoming an Olympic rider.* To me, that basically said it all.

"Your grandma is right," Mom says. "We better get on the ball, Shnoopy. Why don't I leave you and Dean alone for a minute? And, remember, Vivvie, life is about living in the moment. This is *your* moment."

I nod. Since Lane left us, Mom has repeated that saying to me countless times. She claims it is in hopes of helping me be less intense and enjoy the moment—*live in the moment.* I am not always sure if when she says it, it's for my benefit or hers. I have found that living in the moment is not always easy.

I choke back my emotion. Poor Dean doesn't need to see me fall apart. Before I can even look at him, I go first to the stall next to his and wrap my arms around my mom's favorite horse, Bronte (although Mom would never admit that she has faves).

We have four other horses on the property—Chance, Lucy Liu (our miniature), Bronte, and my Dean. All of them are rescues except for Dean. Chance has taught me a lot about trust. Lucy Liu has taught me a few things about determination and willpower. Bronte helps me see the good in everything. And Dean—well, Dean has taught me pretty much everything I know about life.

I kiss Bronte on her nose. I know that the people who had her before she came to live at our house called her "stupid" and worse names than that. They never gave her any respect or love, and they certainly never favored her with her favorite treat, which just happens to be peppermints. Not the hard peppermint candies, but the butter ones that are soft. Dean prefers these apple cookie treats we buy, and Chance is strictly a carrot horse. Believe it or not, Lucy Liu *adores* potato chips—it's about the salt, in her case. It is a strange favorite for a horse, but she *adores* chips. Her word, not mine. The peppermint is too strong for her palate. I know what everyone's favorite treat is, and all sorts of other quirks, likes, and dislikes.

Bronte nuzzles the top of my head, hot air coming through her nostrils. "Hey, cutie. I'm sorry, but with Ren coming down to ride Dean while I'm gone, you're going to have to get used to that music she listens to. Trust me, I don't like it any better than you do. Dean might like it, though. His taste in music isn't as good as ours and Mom's."

I laugh. That was another thing I'll miss about our barn, our horses, and my mom—singing and dancing to music playing from inside the tack room. Our favorite has to be Taylor Swift. She can write and sing a love song! Granted it does seem as if the poor girl has had kind of her share of getting her heart stomped on. Something I want no part of—the heart-stomping thing. Nope. My mind flashes to yesterday and Austen, and that kiss.

"I'll e-mail Ren and tell her to broaden her musical horizons," I tell her. Ren is my twelve-year-old cousin. She lives up the street, and for years she's been wanting to ride Dean. "But you better take care of Mom. Don't let her get too stressed out with Grandma. She's going to need you." I trace the stripe down her face. The mare brushes the side of her face against mine. A picture of her nuzzling my mother comes to mind, followed by one of my cousin Ren feeding her the peppermint treats.

*Don't you worry. I'll take care of your mother. I can handle the music. All I need are some peppermints.*

I scratch between her eyes.

*I love that. I'll miss that.*

A tightness forms in my chest. "I'll tell Ren to be sure she scratches you right there."

*Thank you. You're a good girl.*

"I got you fooled." I laugh.

Okay, so here comes the not-normal part about me—I have this gift or ability or skill. Ever since I can remember, since my mother started taking me on vet calls with her when I was, like, five, I *can* talk to horses . . . and they talk back. No, they don't actually open their mouths and speak to me like I would to my mom or a friend. I *can* read their minds and sense their emotions. They usually show me what they are thinking or feeling in pictures—like in photos or even a movie. Sometimes I can actually feel their pain, grief, even joy, in a physical sense. And I can translate all of that into words.

I work hard to pay attention to what they are saying, and I've kind of given them voices. I know that Bronte's voice sounds sweet, gentle, almost little-girl-like. Somehow it's easy for me to not only see what they want me to see but also hear what they want me to hear.

I know it sounds strange, but it's true. Thus, my occasional outings with Mom on a call. I've saved a few horses from early death, just like Summer. That's not to sound conceited. It's just a fact, but it isn't a fact I share with others—not even with Gail, Mia, Kate, or Austen. Only Mom knows. If anyone found out that I can actually telepathically communicate with these amazing animals, well, I might be locked away in some mental hospital. That would definitely suck. At the very least, I believe I wouldn't exactly be popular in the way most seventeen-year-old girls want to be popular. Not that I'm all that popular, but I do plan to keep the friends I have. So I do my best to make sure no one knows that I'm a regular Dr. Doolittle. But it's only with horses—kind of makes it even weirder. I mean I'd think that if I could talk with horses that I could talk with other animals, but nope. Nothing. I get zip from dogs, cats, rabbits, whatever. It's just me and the horses.

I stroke Bronte along the length of her neck. "Take care of my guy there." I point to Dean's stall.

I sniffle and take in a deep breath. The earthen smells of fresh shavings, hay, manure, and of course my favorite scent—horse—calms my nerves. Dean is watching us from his stall.

I give Bronte one last pat on her neck, latch her stall, and open Dean's. I sigh heavily and bite back those damn tears again.

*I'll miss you, too, kid.*

There is an actual tear in his eye. Yes, horses can cry, too. I reach up and scratch behind his ears—his special spot. He lowers his head for me. "I'm sorry. It's hard. I mean, who am I going to talk to, confide in?" Dean rubs his face against my chest. "Hey, don't get me dirty."

*I'll be here when you come home. Right here. Running the show.*

He shows me a mental image of him, snorting and galloping at full speed through the pasture, his dark tail flaming up in the air, the other horses watching him in awe. I laugh. "Yes, you will."

*Now you go. Be good. Love your new horse. Go live in the moment.*

My throat tightens. "You've been listening too much to Mom."

*Your mom is smart.*

Like me, Dean doesn't do emotion real well. It's what's made us such a good team—a winning team. We understand each other. We're totally in sync. But I can't take him to LA with me. For one thing, he's too old to compete at the levels I'm shooting for. At twenty, he's left his best days behind him.

"Ren will be good to you," I assure him. "She's a good little rider, and sweet. She's so excited about riding you and taking care of you. You'll love her."

*Not like I love you.*

Dean and me—together through the years—jumping jumps, scoring well in dressage tests, and flying through cross-country courses. A kiss on his nose, and an apple or two at the end of a ride. I wrap my arms tight around him and kiss his face again. "I have to go. I'll be home at Christmas. We'll go on trail rides, and I'll bring home lots of apple cookies, and . . ." I sob. "I gotta go."

I leave his stall, and as I walk out of the barn, he trots out to his run. There, he can see me walk to the truck where my mom, grandma, and brother are waiting. I swallow hard and wipe my tears with the back of my hand.

A fog rolls in off the mountains, weaving in and out of the fir trees and lush green landscape that I've loved and known all of my life. A slight drizzle mists down on me. Dean's whinny echoes off the Cascade Mountains as I open the truck door and climb inside. As our truck pulls away, I press my hands to the window and watch him for as long as I can. With the truck's tires crunching on the gravel of our long driveway, my brother's game device making stupid noises in the background, and my grandma already telling my mother what they need to pick up at the store after they drop me off, I silently promise Dean that I'll make him proud.

CHAPTER *four*

In LA, I am picked up by Kayla Fairmont, owner/president/principal—I'm not really sure what to call her. She introduces herself simply as Kayla. Kind of informal, but formalities are typically reserved for the show ring.

We are on the freeway in her black Range Rover. "We're very excited to have you join us, Vivienne. You really blew everyone away with your video and application. We also spoke with your instructors in Oregon. You've racked up some impressive accomplishments."

I shift slightly in the plush leather seating.

"With your show record and your school grades, we felt that you are the perfect fit for the scholarship."

"Thank you." Heat rises to my cheeks. Mom says I need to work on taking compliments better and to just respond with a thank-you. "I'm really grateful for this opportunity." I turn to face Kayla. She is pretty in that California-blonde tan way, thirtysomething. She looks like a rider. There *is* a look. Her long hair is pulled back taut.

She has on a pink polo—polo shirts are big in the horse world—and a pair of breeches and riding boots.

"Sorry about my clothes. I didn't realize how late it was. I was giving a lesson to Martina Lunes, who is actually going to be your roommate. She's a nice kid. I think you'll like her."

"Great." I hope she doesn't hear the hesitation in my voice. The faces of my best friends at home flash through my mind. Having one of them as a roommate would have been something I could get excited about. But all this not knowing . . . I am a creature of habit, and one who likes what she knows. The unknown? It tends to throw me for a loop.

"You'll have some great instructors. And I was happy to see that for your extra curriculum you signed up for barn management. We usually only get a handful of kids in that class, and I think it's one of our best courses. Your teacher, Tanner Bromley, is great. You'll see." She smiles.

We pull up to the front gate at Fairmont, and my jaw drops into my lap. One word—WOW! I had seen the photos in the brochure but, like, seriously *crazy wow!* "This place is insane!"

"We think so, too." Kayla laughs. "We hope you'll love it here. We have two jump arenas, two dressage arenas, twenty-five acres dedicated to our cross-country courses, four paddocks, and two pastures, plus four barns that hold twenty-five horses each. I can't wait to show you around. And out on the back forty we have a really neat old stable house that we call Olympic House. It's got photos of all the past US Olympians and their horses. It's a special place, although students don't go out there much because it is a hike."

"I'd love to see it. My God, this place is so huge. How do you find everything? And there's a view of the ocean!" I look back at the deep blue coastline stretched out behind us. *Incredible.*

The ocean and the beach equals incredible bikinis and bikini body watchers (yep—guys). This will be a problem. I am super pale. An image of surfer gods and goddesses with perfectly sculpted bronze bodies, riding along on their perfectly gorgeous steeds while their perfect golden hair blows in the wind, pops into my head. And then there's me. A melanin-deprived ghost girl.

"Not bad, huh?" says Kayla. "And don't worry. You'll learn your way around quickly."

I can't stop staring. As we proceed up the drive, on either side are the pastures where some of the most amazing horses I have ever seen are grazing. All at least sixteen hands, muscular—definitely warmbloods, Thoroughbreds, sport horses—jumpers and combined training horses. Grays, bays, chestnuts, all just totally beautiful, their coats gleaming in the bright sunlight.

My mind suddenly becomes a mixture of noise and cluttered thoughts—horses' thoughts. Images flash through at a rapid clip. One doesn't like the mare on the left side of her, and as I gaze out the window I see that horse kick out at the other one. Another thinks the grass tastes off today. One horse is just as happy as can be and loves the sun on his back. This is so weird—I've only ever received one horse's thoughts at a time, and usually only after I'd been exposed to that horse. My vision blurs a little and I feel dizzy. I suck in a deep breath.

"You okay?" Kayla looks over at me. "You look a little pale."

"Yeah. I . . ."

"I know, it's a lot to take in, isn't it?" She pats my hand. "Relax.

You're going to do great here. This will be like home away from home before you know it."

*Home.* The mention makes me immediately think about Dean.

We pull up in front of the academy. This place looks nothing like home. The school and its outbuildings have this kind of Tuscan style. Mom has this thing about Italy, and it's her dream for us to go there one day. She's got all of these framed posters in the house of Tuscan villas, hills, vineyards. Green climbing vines with little white flowers intertwine up the sides of one building's stone walls. The main school building is a couple of stories high and looks larger than I thought it would be. "How many kids go here?"

"We are at one fifty-seven right now and never admit more than two hundred. We couldn't incorporate the riding into the curriculum if that was the case. We work with no more than fifty per grade. You being a junior, you actually have the smallest class. There are thirty of you, and then you split off into individual class size, which in itself is no more than twelve in core classes. All very specialized, and schedules vary. You'll see how it works. Not everyone is at the same level of riding ability, so not everyone rides six days a week, as you will."

"Oh."

"School days run from seven until seven. And by school days I mean not only will you have regular classes, you'll also have riding lessons in there, too. You'll rotate dressage, cross-country, and stadium jumping, and we'd like for you to schedule a private session at least once a week in the area in which you, and your instructors, feel you and your horse need the most work. I'll go over your schedule with you after you have a look at your dorm."

I take a second look at the school and am surprised to notice that the flags are at half-mast. "How come the flags . . ."

Kayla swallows hard. "Are at half-mast?" She nods. "We had a death here at the academy about a week ago. A freak accident. Dr. Serena Miller. She was our on-staff vet. Wonderful woman. She was my husband's cousin."

Kayla's eyes fill with tears. "I'm so sorry."

"Thank you. We're going to miss her." She gets out of the SUV and goes around back.

"Oh hey! Kayla! I can help. Luggage, right?"

I turn around to see who is asking. *Mmmm.* Stomach drop. Yeah. Cute guy. No. Not simply cute, but like insanely hot. Really, really hot. And the best part is, he obviously rides. Right? Right. Because this is a riding academy and he has on a pair of breeches, riding boots, and a white polo that is exposing just enough of his golden, strong chest. Surfer god on horseback *does* exist. I blink several times, feeling like an idiot, and then I yell at myself from the inside. *Stop staring at Mister Gorgeous Green Eyes, all muscle, tan, dark hair, like so perfectly hot, and I am not here to check out hot, sexy guys!* A fleeting second passes where I recall Austen and that kiss. Am I forgetting him already? *No!*

"Thanks, Riley. This is . . ."

"I know. Hi, Vivienne," he says.

He shakes my hand, which is super clammy. Gross—not his hand. Mine. He is probably thinking how lame I am. I swallow hard. "Hi. Yes. I'm Vivienne Taylor." *Good. Remembering my name is good.*

"Riley Reed. Pleasure to meet you, too. *You* are the talk of the school." He smiles. A perfect, perfectly white, straight-teeth smile.

*Thank God, my braces came off last year. Thank God.* "Oh?"

"Riley, let poor Vivienne get her foot in the door before you start in on her." She glances sympathetically at me, while Riley pulls my bags out of the back. "Students always want to know who received the scholarship. It's just, well, it's a curiosity thing. You'll be fine. The kids are great here. Everyone is great here."

I cringe. I don't want to be a *curiosity thing*.

"Follow me," Kayla says. "Riley, just set her bags at the front office. And I think Emily is on for today's welcome liaison and handler."

Riley sidles up next to me and lowers his voice. "She exaggerates. You'll see. Not everyone is *great* here. Watch your back, baby." Then he winks at me, and it isn't in a *I think you're cute way*.

Ooh. Some welcome. And with that, Prince Hotness turns into His Royal Jerkness.

# RILEY

## CHAPTER *five*

*So, that's her?*

Riley watches the new girl walk away with Kayla. Whispers of Vivienne Taylor had already made the rounds when the word that she'd received the Fairmont Scholarship spread like wildfire through the halls and in text messages. Most of the students had probably already watched her riding videos on YouTube, sizing up the new competition.

Riley has watched them, too. In his estimation, Vivienne Taylor is indeed worthy of the scholarship. Everyone knows that scholarship kids tend to be different than most of the other students at the academy. They are more driven, more focused—they are the riders to beat. And . . . they do not usually thrive at Fairmont. Unless . . . they either become *less* focused and driven, or they have something else to offer—an "in" to the in crowd.

*Will this new girl offer anything extra, or will we all drive her away?*

Riley drops Vivienne's bags at the front office. Emily Davenport, whose family comes from ancient money and whose mother lives vicariously through the poor girl, stands at the whiteboard checking off the students who have already arrived.

"New girl on campus, Em," Riley says.

"Super," Emily replies. She turns around from the board. Her light brown hair is plaited into two thick braids against her shoulders. She looks at him with large blue eyes. "I hate this place."

"Why are you here, then?" he asks.

She tilts her head to the side. "Why are you here, then?" She sets the marker down and looks at Vivienne's luggage. "Oh God, how Walmart can we be? Scholarship girl?"

"Obvs."

"Fine. I'll get the bags dropped at the *special rider's* room."

"Thanks, Em. Hang in there. It could be worse."

"Really, Riley? Really? Could it?"

"Yeah, Em, it could," he mutters as he exits the office and sets off toward the barns.

He is walking past the pastures when he hears someone call out his name. Nate Deacon. Nate Deacon is one of those guys who seems to have it all—looks, brains, riding ability, charm with the girls, money, and more. But Riley thinks that the guy is also kind of a sociopath.

"Hey, Reed-man, wait up." He jogs over to Riley.

They do the "bro" thing with the high fives.

"How was your summer?" Nate asks.

"It was okay."

"I was here for the summer. My parents went to their house in Cannes. I didn't want to hang there with them."

Riley chuckles. "Right."

"Unbelievable what happened with Dr. Miller."

"Yeah. Pretty messed up," Riley replies. "I didn't see you at her service."

"Nah, man. I don't do funerals. Creep me out."

Riley nods impatiently.

"You meet the new girl?" Nate asks.

"Just unloaded her stuff. Em is liaison today."

Nate smiles his greasy-oily smile. "I like me some Emily Davenport."

"Isn't she a bit of a downer?" Riley comments.

"Yeah. Makes her easy prey. I like to give her spirits a *rise*."

"I really gotta—"

"Anyway, the new chick," Nate says. "What's her name . . ." He snaps his fingers.

"Vivienne."

"Right. Vivienne. Ready for a new new-girl initiation?"

Riley shakes his head.

"Come on. Shannon loved it. Sorry you got my hand-me-down."

Riley frowns.

The Scholarship Girl Game initiation started a few years back. The first three guys to meet the new girl are the "tap-it" guys, meaning that whichever of them can get the new girl to have sex with them, receives the winnings from the bet. The other guys on campus put cash into betting on one specific contestant.

Shannon Burton is the most recent girl to receive the scholarship, and Nate is the first guy she met. He won the bet. That was two years ago. Shannon now has her sights set on Riley.

"I saw her YouTube video. She looks hot. And since you already met her . . . nice going, by the way. You are one of three. And, my friend, I plan to be number two on that list."

"I don't know. She seems like a 'nice' girl."

"They're all nice girls. And even nicer underneath you."

Riley starts walking toward the barn. "I don't think so," he says.

Nate slaps him on the back. "Two weeks. You got two weeks to get in on the bet and the semester to score. I bet you change your mind. The pool is already at five hundred and it is going to go up-up-up."

"Not interested."

"You do what you want, Ri. I am off to meet one Miss Vivienne Taylor."

*Douchebag walking.* Riley watches Nate saunter away.

Riley shakes off Nate's disgustingness and gets his horse Santos out and ready for his afternoon dressage lesson.

In the tack room, he runs into Alicia Vincenzia—a royal pain in the butt—and her sidekick Shannon. Shannon's "in" to the in crowd is that she is drop-dead gorgeous. She wound up being Nate's girlfriend for a semester last year, before she decided that Riley was a better catch. Alicia on the other hand, is from old East Coast money, and is cute at best. Money has bought her designer clothes and a nose job, but hasn't fixed her bitchy personality.

"Hey, Alicia," he says.

"Oh, hi, Ri. How's it going?" Alicia asks, pulling her long black hair into a ponytail and grabbing her helmet off one of the hanging racks.

"I'm good. You've got a lesson, too?" he asks.

"Yeah. Fun stuff with Holden."

"Hmm. No, kidding. What about you?" He turns his eye to Shannon.

"Do I look like I'm riding this afternoon?" She tosses her shoulder-length brown hair, and straightens the hemline of her short skirt.

" I just thought maybe you hadn't changed yet." Riley picks up his brush box and starts back out to groom Santos, who is standing patiently in the cross ties.

"I came to watch *your* lesson today," she replies, batting her lashes fiercely over her blue eyes. Riley's stomach sinks. Shannon Burton is definitely one of the hot girls, and they've even made out. But she's really not Riley's type.

"I like watching you ride." She smiles suggestively.

Alicia giggles. "I think most of us do." She grins at Riley, who feels his face burn.

When he doesn't respond, Shannon follows him. Riley begins brushing Santos down.

"Where were you at lunch today? Lydia and all of us were wondering."

He swipes the bristles against the horse's coat. "Oh, you know, I had some stuff to do, then I ran into Kayla and the new girl."

"The new girl?" Shannon crosses her arms. "The scholarship girl?"

"Ooh, fascinating." Alicia comes out of the tack room, fastening her helmet strap. "What's she like?"

"Oh, I don't know," he replies. "Seems okay."

"Only okay?" Shannon asks snottily.

"Uh-oh, jealousy alert," Alicia snorts.

"Am not."

Riley so wants out of here.

"Maybe you should be," Alicia replies. "They haven't given out many scholarships and if I remember right, you were the last one to get one, Shan. Lucky to keep it, too."

"Don't be such a bitch."

"So, really, Ri, what is the new girl like?" Alicia persists.

Riley turns and heads back into the tack room to get his saddle pad and saddle. "I told you that I don't know. She seems *okay*."

"Is she hot? Pretty? Stupid? How did she dress? You know she's poor if she needed the scholarship," Alicia says and opens the door on the stall where her mare Lilah is kept.

"Hey, my family isn't exactly poor," Shannon protests.

Alicia laughs and hollers back as she enters her horse's stall, "Don't be so sensitive. Sure, I guess your family isn't poor by normal standards, but around here . . ."

"Lay off, Alicia," Riley says.

Shannon mouths *thank you* and smiles at him.

*God! Why did I do that?*

"C'mon, Shan, we love you. You know that. You're one of us. But the new girl? I'm waiting, Riley . . . what is she *like*?" Alicia walks out of the stall with Lilah on a lead rope.

"Like a *girl*. She seems like a very nice girl who no doubt has worked her ass off to get here. Maybe you two should chill for once. Does every day have to be a bitchfest?" Unhooking the cross ties, Riley's slides the bit into Santos's mouth, slipping the bridle on and over his ears.

"God, Ri. What's up with you? We just want some info," Alicia says as Riley leads Santos out of the barn and over to the mounting block.

"I know you guys better than that. You're already planning to harass the new girl. Why don't you try being nice for a change? Retract the claws."

Shannon and Alicia, are left speechless by this very unexpected demand.

On the back of Santos and heading out to the dressage ring, it hits him. Once Lydia Gallagher—queen bitch of the bitches—gets wind of the conversation he's just had with Alicia and Shannon, Vivienne Taylor's life will be turned into a living hell. On top of that, he knows Nate will pursue her with a vengeance. He hopes that the look in Vivienne's eyes when he met her is reflective of who she really is. She is going to need that type of grit and fierceness to survive this place.

# CHAPTER *six*

OMG. Matz Hall. This *has* to be a good sign. Kayla and I walk through the halls of the dorm named after the most successful show jumper ever. Wasn't a rich kid, came from a regular family. Made it to three Olympics, medaled in the World Equestrian Championships, won the team gold medal in the World Championships. And then he becomes this incredible trainer—and a hero! The guy saved three kids when the plane they were all on crashed near Sioux City, Iowa. Who does stuff like that? Heroes do!

But then I look around a little bit more, and I notice this: *everyone* is staring at me. Guys, girls, even some adults take a long look—kind of like one of those teen movies where the new girl arrives and gets the major up-and-down once-over. I am sweating at my bra line at this point. I grew up with practically the same group of kids since kindergarten. I've never been the new kid. And I'm definitely not in Albany, Oregon, anymore.

Kayla pulls me out of my thoughts. "Because we have a year-round program, a lot of the kids—especially those whose families live close by—tend to spend part of their summer vacation at home. We'll be full up by late afternoon tomorrow, but some lessons have already started. My husband, Holden, is out teaching a dressage lesson right now. I should tell you—he seems like a tough guy when you first meet him, but he's hardest on those who he thinks have the most potential. And you, Ms. Taylor, arrive with some pretty steep expectations."

*Oh.* "How steep?"

She wraps an arm around my shoulders and laughs. "Don't worry. I just mean that you're good. And scrutiny and pressure are things any future Olympian has to get used to."

*Future Olympian.* Those words coming from Kayla Fairmont. I cannot even respond.

And now I notice the whispers. As soon as I walk past, I hear in hushed tones things like *"Is that the new girl? I wonder if she's really all that good"*—and yes, most of the chatter is done among those who are indeed tan and golden with perfect hair, perfect body, perfect clothes. Perfectly perfect.

One perfect guy stops us as we head to my room. "Hi, Kayla." He smiles at me. This one has dark hair, dark eyes, and ridiculously white teeth. What planet have I landed on?

"Hi, Nate. Nate Deacon, this is Vivienne Taylor."

He turns to me and smiles. "Vivienne. Hi. It's so nice to meet you. Can I help you with anything?"

"No. I don't think so."

"Emily will be bringing her bags up."

"Good. Good. Emily's a great girl," he says. Now he is walking with us. "It is awesome here, Vivienne."

"It seems to be."

"Aren't you in Mr. Bromley's barn management class this year, Nate?" Kayla asks.

He frowns at this. "Yeah. I couldn't get the art of horses class that I wanted for my extracurricular."

"That is a popular one. Vivienne here is actually in barn management."

"Really? Terrific. We can study together. I hear it's a tough class."

"O . . . kay."

"I can show you around campus if you like," he says.

Why is this Nate guy being so nice? I mean he's cute and all, but he is just a little too *much*. "I'm kind of tired."

"We should let Vivienne get settled in first," Kayla says.

"Absolutely." He takes a piece of paper and a pen from his pocket, writes something, and hands it to me. "Here's my number if you need anything. I have a lesson anyway, but for you, I'd totally give it up."

*He would?* Cute—yes. Over the top—definitely. "Thanks." I force a smile.

"See you soon."

I'm both dizzy and relieved to see him go.

Kayla laughs. "Nate is a bit of a ladies' man."

"Hmm. Yeah. I think I got that."

"He's harmless."

"Good."

We take the elevator to the fourth floor.

"The guys are on the first two floors, and the girls get the better view on the top two. I had a part in making that happen."

"The view?" I ask.

"You'll see." Kayla takes out a key and unlocks the door.

I stand there like an idiot, staring. *Am I dreaming?* When I realize I might be drooling, I shut my mouth and take a step inside. "Emily should be up with your luggage shortly."

I nod in my oddly numb state. Again, one word, same word: *wow*. Or I'll even go a bit further this time: OMG, and yes, I do know that is an acronym for three words. HGTV would be impressed by this room—correction, *suite*.

"Your roommate should be up soon. Then whenever you're ready, just take a look on the map or ask someone where my office is, and I'll take you down to the barn and have you meet your new partner," Kayla says.

My eyes grow big. "My horse?" Part of being accepted on scholarship means that if you didn't have a horse to bring with you, the academy provides one.

She smiles. "That's right. Harmony's a very pretty gray mare. You could go and meet her on your own, if you'd like," Kayla says. "Name plates are on the stall doors. Map is on your desk." She points to a glass-topped desk with a large envelope on it. "That's your intake info. Why don't you review it, rest a bit, meet Harmony, and then come see me and I can give you a real tour. By that time we'll be about ready for dinner. We're also having a movie night tonight, if you're up for it."

I so already love Kayla. It's like she can read my mind. I do want to meet my new horse by myself for the first time. "Thanks."

As she opens the door to leave, another girl appears with my luggage, looking none too pleased at carrying it. "Oh, good. Emily Davenport, meet Vivienne Taylor," Kayla says.

"Hi," I reply.

"Here's your stuff. Welcome."

"Emily . . ." Kayla gives her a look that reminds me of one of my mother's don't-go-there looks.

Emily smiles now and chirps. "Sorry. I'm just a little tired. Anyway, glad to have you at Fairmont."

Okay, that was about as fake as the "Rolex" watch my grandma brought home from a recent trip to New York. Or am I just being cynical? Maybe all the whispering in the hall has gotten to me. I smile back at her and say, "Thanks."

Kayla clasps her hands together. "Em, I say we let Vivienne get settled in. Tonight's movie and tomorrow's student mixer aren't mandatory, but they're good ways to meet people. See you soon."

"Yes. Thanks again, Kayla, and thank you, Emily, for bringing up my bags."

I hold back a squeal until I think they are far enough down the hall. "Oh my God. Oh my God. Oh my God!" I do a little twirly celebration dance like Julie Andrews in *The Sound of Music* when she's singing about the hills being alive (Mom's favorite movie; watching it has become an annual event in our house).

*Mom.*

She would so die to see this. There are two rooms. One has one of those circular couches all in black, and a couple of cool chairs spaced around a coffee table, also in black. On top of that, there are two desks, and a stereo in the bookcase! No visible TV, but seriously, who will have time for TV in this place? The bedroom has twin beds, dressers painted white—that black and white theme is going on everywhere in the room, and there are pencil sketches on the wall, of course of horses. But the best part—I have a view of the ocean. The Pacific Ocean! I can look out my window and see horses grazing in the pastures and then beyond that is the ocean! Oh my God. I have died and gone to horse heaven, or some kind of heaven.

I am really at Fairmont, and this is really an opportunity of a lifetime. I am going to seize every second of this. The adrenaline rushes through me. I want to meet my horse.

I take a look at myself in the mirror. *Shudder.* Oh, so not good. I sigh. I don't do makeup well, so I rarely wear it, but I'd figured that today, flying to Los Angeles—my big day and all—I'd at least do some mascara, blush, and lip gloss. Lip gloss has long worn off, blush looks okay because there wasn't much there anyway, but the mascara has run underneath my eyes—my supposedly best asset, according to Grandma. My big blue eyes. That's how she talks about me to friends: *Oh my granddaughter with the big blue eyes.* Oh God. Running mascara. How did that happen? I must've rubbed my eyes after I woke up from a nap on the plane. I look like a . . . a small-town girl who doesn't know how to wear makeup and is clueless about fashion or anything remotely cool. Riley saw me like this! A ton of kids saw me like this! And my hair. I take out a rubber band from my purse, pull back my hair, scrub my face, and put on a new T-shirt.

As I get closer to the barns, the noises that I'd heard pulling into the property start again. My head jams with thoughts of carrots, spurs, crops, kids, baths—some horses like them and some don't—and jumping, cantering, hurting, feeling good. If a horse is having a thought, I am hearing all about it, yet I can't tell from which horses the thoughts are coming.

I stand in the center of the padded aisle of the barn that Harmony is stalled in. The barns are as pristine and beautiful as everything else on the campus, but I can't take any of it in. Not really. All I'm able to do is try and shut the thoughts out. I close my eyes and shake my head. Why is this happening? I've never, ever had anything like this happen before. Thoughts from the horses have always been organized. I knew who they came from, and I never picked up more than one horse's thoughts at a time. I finally yell out, "Stop!" The horses down the row I'm on turn their heads and peer at me.

A middle-aged guy wearing a baseball cap and riding attire comes out from one of the stalls. "Excuse me?"

"Oh. Hi. I didn't know anyone was here. I'm sorry. I'm trying to find my horse."

He steps forward and stretches out his hand. "New student, I'm guessing? I'm Newman Becker."

"No way." How did I not recognize him? I guess because the hair sticking out from under his cap is now mostly gray, and he has a few lines on his face that weren't there when I saw him on TV in the 2000 Olympics. Newman Becker rode jumpers. I knew he was an instructor at Fairmont. "It's so great to meet you," I say, gushing and rambling. "I mean you're, wow, you are Newman Becker."

He flashes his famous smile. "I am. And you are?"

"I'm Vivienne Taylor."

"Vivienne. Scholarship Vivienne. Nice going, kid."

"Thanks."

"You and I will be doing quite a bit of work together. I was going over my roster, and I've got your group in the arena on Tuesday and Thursday afternoons."

I'm going to be taking lessons from Newman Becker! "Great." It is great. It really is, but holy crap. Newman Becker. "So great."

"So why were you yelling 'stop'?" he asks.

I wince. "I . . . I was kind of stressing, and I was yelling at myself." That was sort of the truth. I wasn't really yelling at the horses, and since I'd started talking with Newman, I hadn't been picking up anything from my four-legged friends.

"Huh. I can see how all of this newness might stress you out. You're riding Harmony, right?"

"I am."

"She's a fabulous mare."

That was all he was going to give me about the horse? "Where is she?"

"Around the corner and up three stalls. Want me to show you?"

"I'm good. Thanks."

"Okay. I'm sure I'll see you before Tuesday. Nice to meet you, Viv."

"You, too."

I half-skip around the corner. I just met Newman Becker, who called me Viv, which usually I would not like, especially if I didn't know the person, but come on, he was an Olympian! He could call me dumbass and I'd be totally cool with that.

Taking in the barn—its well-lit breezeway and cherry-paneled stall doors with placards bearing the names of the horses inside each stall—I can't wipe the silly smile off my face. There is not even a drop of manure on the ground. I think the barns at Fairmont are probably cleaner than my room back home, and I am not a slob.

As I round the corner, some of the noise starts again. I begin to hum, which helps. I hum "I'm Just a Girl." Who knew that Gwen Stefani's voice in my mind would shut out who wanted carrots and who wanted me to go away and who wanted me to come and say hello?

When I get to Harmony's stall, the thoughts and images are quieting, with only one or two here and there, and I can tell where they are coming from. Harmony is outside in her run and seems to have no interest in turning around and greeting me.

The bay gelding on the other side, though, definitely wants a hello, and the chestnut gelding on the opposite side is hoping I have some kind of treat called a Start-to-Finish, and he specifically wants an apple, not a carrot, and he specifically wants that brand. I glance at him and get the feeling that Sebastian—his name is on the stall—has an OCD issue. I don't let on that I'm on to him. I'm not ready to open that door yet. I want to establish a connection with my new horse first.

"Here, mare." I kiss and cluck. I call her name. "Harmony. Hi girl. Hey. Hi." Nothing. She does a sort of half turn with her neck and then goes back to looking out of her run. I hope she isn't sick.

She is one of the most beautiful horses that I have ever seen. I unlatch her stall door and walk in. Still nothing. Sebastian, though, is fervently hoping I have those treats, and the bay really wants me to come and say hello. He is bobbing his head and practically yelling at me to give him attention. But Harmony gives me . . . nothing.

She is acting as if I'm not even there as I rub my hands all over her dappled dark-gray body. She stands about sixteen hands. Perfect. Her face is delicate—definitely a mare's face, with a slight dish to her nose. My guess is she is likely a Trakhener. The breed can be a little temperamental. Her muscles are toned and strong and she is at a great weight—a perfect athlete. "Hey, girl, you feel okay?"

Nothing.

An empty silence.

I look into her large dark eyes. Pretty, but . . . vacant. I can't describe them any other way, and it . . . well, it scares me. I take a step back, blink my eyes several times to clear my head. A rush of air escapes from between my lips. Harmony's eyes are empty and blank. It truly does scare the hell out of me. I breathe in deeply, feeling off. What is this horse's story? I've seen angry eyes, kind eyes, eyes filled with fear or pain, but *vacant* is all new to me.

And now noises start again, and it seems as if every horse on the campus is saying something, feeling something, needing something.

Every horse but mine.

And then—a flash of red, dark red, and total panic—and then black.

*Me.*

And everything goes dark.

CHAPTER *seven*

mazing dream. Incredibly amazing godly being is holding me. His eyes are the color of pasture grass, his hair the color of wheat, and his skin is as golden as everyone else's at Fairmont.

Fairmont!

"Vivienne? Hello? You okay?"

I sit up quickly, feeling dizzy all over again, trying to focus, seeing the gray mare—my mare—Harmony in her stall, turning away from me. "Uh, um . . ." I stutter.

"You are Vivienne? Right? Are you okay? What happened?"

"I . . . yeah, I'm Vivienne. How did you know?" I try to stand up. "I'm fine."

"No. No," he says. "I don't think that standing is such a good idea. I should get the school nurse."

"No! Seriously. I am fine." The last thing I need after already being looked at as the freakish scholarship new girl and having

Golden Boy find me passed out in the horse's stall—the horse with the vacant eyes, no less—is to have word get out that I fainted.

"You sure?"

I nod slowly, still absorbing every movement of his lips. "Yes."

He stands up and holds out a hand. "I'm Tristan. I found you here. Passed out. What happened?"

I take his hand and he pulls me up. I stumble, falling into his chest. My body grows hot, and I just know my face is probably magenta.

"Whoa. You sure you're okay?"

I pull myself up straight. "Yes. Hi. Thank you. I flew in earlier today and didn't drink much water and . . ."

"Uh-huh. Okay. I still think you should see the nurse."

"No. I'll . . . lie down for a bit. That'll be good." I am nodding a bit too enthusiastically.

"I'll walk you back to your room." He opens the stall door and I follow him out.

Am I still dreaming? "No. I'm okay."

"I insist," he says. "I just came out to give my horse some carrots and happened to see you passed out." He points to the large chestnut next to Harmony's stall. (Ah! He owns Mr. OCD/Sebastian. What might this say about him?) "I'd heard the new girl's horse would be Harmony." He looks down. "I'm glad she's getting someone to take care of her."

"What do you mean?" I ask.

He looks at me, those green, green eyes so intense and so damn beautiful. "No one told you?"

"Told me what?"

"About Harmony's owner. Dr. Miller?"

"The vet who passed away last week?"

"Harmony was her horse. It was in her will that the horse go to the school in the event of her death."

It suddenly all makes sense. She misses her owner. I start feeling better. It might take a few days, but once I explain to her that I'm here for her, then maybe I can help her recover from her loss and . . . but what if I can't help her? What if I am over my head on this one?

I feel a hand on my shoulder and swing back around. It's Golden Boy. "You sure you're all right?"

"Fine." I look away, feeling my face heat up again. "I'm gonna go now. Thanks for helping me."

"You know, I'd feel a lot better if . . ."

"Tristan!"

We turn around to see a long-haired blond, blue-eyed girl. (Jesus, could someone just please look normal and regular here in Barbie-and-Ken Land?) She is bouncing—as in braless bouncing—down the barn aisle. Bouncy Barbie practically lights up like a Christmas tree on steroids as she bounces toward us, and I notice Tristan's eyes widen some. He smiles weakly. "Hi, Lydia."

"Hi? Hi. Is that all I get?" Her lips are pink and glossy, her blue eyes expertly rimmed in dark eyeliner. I shift uneasily. I mean, this girl is really pretty. "You don't see me all summer and I get a 'hi'? How are things at home? I mean, I know how they *were*." She smirks. "All those texts and e-mails. You are such a bad boy!" She smacks his chest lightly.

First I faint. Now will I barf?

"I hope you saved some of that naughtiness for me."

Speechless. Me. Totally.

She turns her shiny self toward me. "Oh. New girl. Hello. Welcome. I'm Lydia Gallagher."

I shake her manicured hand and can't help wondering how in the world she rides with these nails.

"Lydia, this is Vivienne."

"Oh. *Oh.* That explains it. The scholarship girl. Nice going. Rumor has it you are very talented. We should have a little fun competing this year."

"Right, so what do you mean, *that explains it?*" I ask.

She giggles and waves a hand. "Oh, nothing. Nothing that can't be fixed."

I cross my arms and eyeball her. "I'm confused."

She points at my clothing. "I'm sorry. That won't do."

"Lydia," Tristan says, his tone tinged with warning.

"What? I'm only trying to help the new girl out."

"Thanks. I don't need your particular kind of help." I turn and start walking back down the barn aisle. "Thank you again, Tristan."

When I am obviously still in earshot I hear Lydia say: "Wow, she's a little *interesting*. And she definitely needs my help."

"You coming to movie night?" Tristan hollers after me.

I turn back around and catch a death glare from Lydia. "I'm not sure."

"If you come tonight, we can save you a seat."

He seems awkward, and I definitely feel awkward as Lydia locks her fingers around his and leans possessively against him.

On the walk back to my room I am thinking: What in the hell have I gotten myself into by coming to Fairmont?

TRISTAN

CHAPTER *eight*

"Wﾍat was that all about?" Lydia spouts as soon as Vivienne is out of the breezeway. She grips Tristan's hand tighter.

"What was what all about?" he asks, his stomach twisting into a knot.

"The new girl? We'll save *you* a seat at movie night? Um, yeah . . . no. Think I have some opinions here."

He sighs. "Why do you have to be like that? I mean, really? She seems like a nice girl and she's new. Why can't you just be a little more decent to people outside your clique?"

She drops his hand and crosses her arms. "Are you serious? That girl would never fit in with us. She's *so* average."

"Not as a rider." Truthfully, Tristan hasn't found Vivienne Taylor to be average in any way. Not at all. Long, dark-reddish hair, amazing blue eyes. Beautiful. Not glamour-girl beautiful like Lydia, but unique.

And he can appreciate unique.

"Oh no, don't tell me you find that girl hot?" She approaches him and places her hands on his chest, looks up at him. "Come on, T. Me and you are who everyone here dreams of being. I didn't mean to be nasty, but honestly, you know as well as I do that that girl won't fit in." She moves her hands up around his neck and slicks her fingers through the short ends of his hair.

Tristan closes his eyes. *God, she is impossible to ignore.*

Lydia backs him up against one of the stall doors, tracing a finger down his chest. "You know, I think we should make good on some of our texts over the summer. The things we *said* we wanted to do." She raises her eyebrows. "I missed you. A lot." Her hands move all over him and he can't resist putting his around her waist, then inching them up underneath her shirt.

"I missed you, too," he finally says.

She smiles up at him. "And after what you told me . . . the secret. I knew that you must really trust me. For you to share what . . ."

"I don't want to talk about that."

"I understand. I am just happy you felt you could tell me."

He swallows hard. He'd had a weak moment over the summer and confided something to Lydia. Something that, if it ever got out, would ruin his family.

*How stupid could I be?*

"Well, since you feel like you can trust me with your deepest, darkest secrets. I think I can trust you with something of mine."

"Mm-hmm," he replies

"I, uh . . . I just got the pill, so it'll take like a month, but then . . ."

What is there to say? He likes her. Except the fact that she can be a first-class bitch, like she had been toward Vivienne. She is hot like no one else at the school. And, they'd been together for about a month before school ended last year and she had to head back home to Georgia. And, yeah, they had texted all summer and e-mailed, and the things they'd "talked" about doing . . . "You did?" he finally asks.

"I want our first time to be special. I made some plans. Homecoming is only a few weeks away, and I thought that maybe after the dance we could get away," she says.

"To where?"

"How about the Olympic House? No one ever goes there."

"But, it's kind of . . . old. I've never thought of it as, uh, romantic."

She bats her eyelashes. "That's where you come in. You will make it nice in there for our special night, and I will make everything very nice for you."

He clears his throat, trying hard to ignore the heat traveling through him.

"I have to go now. I have a jump lesson. I'll see you tonight." She turns and saunters away.

Tristan shakes his head and lets out a long shuddery sigh. Somehow as Lydia walks away, Vivienne Taylor enters his mind and he can't help wondering if she's really okay. *God, is he being a total ass? Is he really that guy?*

He starts back to his room and runs smack dab into Nate Deacon. Over the years at Fairmont, Nate has tried to convince everyone that Tristan and he are best buddies. Tristan keeps the guy at arm's length because if you don't play nice with him, Nate will figure out a way to make life a bit of a hell for you.

"Hey, T. How's it going?"

"Good. Just heading up to my room."

"Right. By the way, congrats on being number three," Nate says.

"Excuse me?"

"You, my friend, are lucky number three. I followed little Red down here, and gotta say she is a hot one. Kind of weird, though. Saw her yell at the horses just before Becker intro'd himself. Then, when she passed out, you were right there, Prince Charming? Nice move."

Tristan shoves his hands into his pockets. "What? What the hell are you talking about? You saw Vivienne faint in the stall?"

"Riley met her when she first arrived and then I made it a point to meet her next. Then, I decided to put the scope on her. Give her a little follow and see who number three might be. You are it. Oh, and nice with Lydia. You got that all tied up, don't you?"

Tristan shakes his head. "First off, it's creepy that you followed her, and then watched me try and help her. Then you watched me with Lydia?"

"I only saw your chick wrap her arms around you. It wasn't like I'm all Mister Peeping Tom. I let you two kids have your moment. I watched Red hike back to her dorm. Mmm. Nice fresh new ass."

"Listen, I'm not 'it' or in. The bet is stupid."

"Riley doesn't think so. He is definitely in."

"I don't believe that."

"Well, he will be," Nate says. "Just like you will be, too."

"Forget it. Forget her. Good-bye, Nate."

*Ass.* Tristan walks back to the dorm with Vivienne Taylor on his mind.

CHAPTER *nine*

I don't make it to movie night for a couple of reasons. First I am completely embarrassed and don't want to run into Golden Boy and Boobie. The second is that I got a horrific headache.

The upside is that I meet my roommate Martina, and she is exactly as Kayla told me she'd be—nice, bright, and funny. We immediately hit it off. And—she's neither golden nor blonde! Her family is Latino and she has dark, shoulder-length hair, deep-brown eyes, and olive skin.

We decide to kick back in our suite and talk. "So, is this place as perfect as it seems?" I ask.

"It's pretty great," she says. "The classes and the lessons are hard, though. It's definitely intense."

"You've been here since you were a freshman?"

"All three years," she replies. "I think the education is great, and our riding lessons are taught by some of the best instructors in the world."

"Why do I hear a 'but' in there?" I ask.

"I love the school and teachers . . ."

"You said that already." I look over at her. Martina casts her eyes downward and crosses her arms, leaning back against the couch. "Let me guess, the social scene is even tougher?"

She nods. "The thing is, you would think that since all of us have our love for horses in common, we would be like one big happy family."

I shake my head. "Not necessarily. Let's face it, unless you are on a country team or ride for one of the clubs, so much of eventing is an individual sport. Sure, we can choose to team-ride, but in reality, we ride to win for ourselves. I would imagine, by just looking around this place this afternoon, that's the vibe—win and take no prisoners." I laugh.

"For a lot of kids here, that is the case," she replies.

"You must have some friends here, though. You've been here going on three years."

She frowns. "My best friend Jules took a bad spill last year out on cross-country. She's actually paralyzed now. She's from Texas, and her parents took her home. I don't know. I have a hard time making friends, I guess."

"Oh my God. I'm so sorry about your friend. That's awful. Is she okay? I mean relatively speaking, I guess." I fumble for the right words.

Martina shrugs. "Jules is tough, and there is some hope for recovery. We e-mail and talk sometimes, but it has been hard on her."

"I am just really sorry."

She musters a smile. "Thanks. And, well, I suppose I don't exactly fit in with some of the kids here. Unless you look like Lydia Gallagher or Emily Davenport . . ."

"Met both of them," I reply.

"You shouldn't have a problem making friends here. You're really pretty."

I automatically make a face at her. "They are so not who I want to hang out with. Speaking of, what's the deal with that guy Tristan?"

She laughs. "Oh, you've met Lydia's guy. Yeah, she's got that poor sucker wrapped so tight around her bitchy little finger."

"I figured. She's so obnoxious."

"But he is hot, isn't he?"

I laugh. "Maybe."

"Oh please, everyone knows he's hot, and everyone knows she's hot, and they're just this gross hot couple."

"And that Riley kid?"

"Look at you. You've noticed all the cuties, haven't you?"

"Actually, he was kind of a jerk to me," I reply.

"Riley's okay. Except he does hang out with Lydia and her people. Shannon Burton has a thing for him. I'm sure you'll meet her. She received the scholarship two years ago and was one of the few 'outsiders' to be inducted in with the popular kids."

"And I met Nate Deacon?"

"Slimeball."

"Obviously," I concur.

After we chow down a pizza, Martina says, "We should probably work those calories off."

"The gym, now?" I ask.

"Nope. You got any favorite singers, bands?"

"No Doubt?"

Martina shakes her head. "Not on my iPod. You like Taylor Swift?"

"Yep!"

She puts on the music, grabs my hand, and starts to dance. At first, I feel silly. "Come on, Vivienne. It's a dance party!"

"Fine." After several minutes of goofing off and looking like a couple of clowns, we plop down on the couch, gasping, and laugh like maniacs. We laugh like Mia and Kate and I do back at home. I twirl the charms on the bracelet they gave me, smiling when I see Austen's charm. I'm relieved that I have at least found one friend here.

Martina finishes giving me the lowdown on the toughest teachers, on how to manage lessons, on campus chores, and a ton more.

We finally say good night, and even though I'm exhausted from the day, I have a hard time falling asleep, my mind on the mare—hopeful that with a new day, I'll receive a different response from her. One that will indicate to me that Harmony and I are going to have a successful partnership, just like Dean and I had.

CHAPTER *ten*

Saturday. The rest of the students are arriving, and the place is busy. With all the activity no one notices me quite as much. I can still sense some looks and whispers, but it isn't as bad as the day before.

Martina has gone back to her house to grab a few more things. I think it's kind of interesting that her family lives only forty-five minutes inland, and yet she lives on campus, but I didn't ask her about this last night.

Kayla Fairmont came by our room this morning and basically insisted that I attend the mixer tonight. She said that it was a good opportunity to get to know some of the other students and that Martina should help make those introductions for me. Martina and I agreed to go, but we aren't exactly excited about it.

I walk toward the barns, feeling the nerves in my stomach, and silently pray that this will be a good day.

I reach Harmony's stall, take the halter off the hook, and unlatch the door. She stands as she did the day before—outside the stall in the far corner of her run. "Hey, girl," I say, walking up to her. I purposely do not look into her eyes. I put the halter on her with ease. I begin to run my hands all over her body, the smells of horse, earth, and hay wafting through the air. She doesn't move as I pet her. She also doesn't have any response to me. Dean would be talking the entire time to me about what he likes, and where he's sore, and on and on. I remind myself that this could take time, and patience is key.

Sebastian tells me once again to come over and pet him and give him his specific treats. Him I hear loud and clear.

I finally come around to Harmony's neck and then her head. I run my hands down the front of her face. That she does not shy away is a good sign. I look into her eyes. The *vacancy* is not there like it had been, but something has replaced it. A sadness, and . . . fear? "What is it, sweet girl? What happened to you? You can tell me. I will understand. I know your owner is gone, and that's probably very confusing for you," I say aloud. Then I think the words. Conjure up images in my mind that, in the past, allowed horses to understand that they were safe with me, and that I understood their need for safety.

Harmony gives me nothing in response.

I put her in the cross ties and groom her. The whole time she maintains her silence. Saddle on, bridle on, my helmet on, and we are ready to go. I get on her over at the mounting block. As soon as I do, something shifts in Harmony. She becomes a nervous ball of energy, prancing and dancing. Her ears prick forward. She jigs to the side and at one point kicks her right hind leg out straight.

I speak in low tones to her. If the horses at home—including

Dean—had behaved like this, they would have first gotten a decent scolding from me. And possibly a crack on the butt with a crop. But I don't know this horse, other than that she has experienced trauma. Losing her owner would have been traumatic itself, but my sense is there might be something more than that. Call it a hunch.

See, every horse has a history—just as we do. And horses have distinct memories of people, in particular. Scientists say that the memory of a horse rivals that of an elephant, which according to the experts is pretty remarkable. If I didn't see Dean for ten years, he would remember me the minute he and I saw each other again. And not because of my "gift." It is simply true of most horses. Each one comes with a unique personality and set of quirks, and like children, their histories help dictate what and who they become as they age.

I have to learn more about this horse's history if I'm ever going to figure her out and become her friend and riding partner.

We ride to the open arena, where I appear to be the only one out on a horse. Considering her squirrelly behavior, this is a good thing.

I put her to work. I put my leg on, relying on the strength of my core muscles for posture and balance, as well as correct breathing, and after a walk around the arena, I ask her for a trot. I'm pleasantly surprised when she moves her hind end nicely up underneath herself, using her muscles properly. Her gait is smooth, and she's round and supple. We move this way around the arena and then cross the diagonal, changing direction. Out of the corner of my eye, I think I see someone watching me. As I make the bend and go long, I see who it is: Tristan. I swallow. He smiles and gives me a little wave.

My body tenses, and the second it does, so does Harmony's, and we fall apart. She flies hard to the left, and then bucks so athletically that the move would have made a rodeo bull proud.

The last time I was bucked off I was seven years old, and it had been this nasty pony who let me know before I ever climbed on his back that he hated me because I was not his original kid. He only wanted her. Foolish me, I only wanted that cute pony. Yeah. That didn't work out so well. And neither did that moment on Harmony's back, because 1 went flying off.

Stunned and on the ground, I see hooves race past me. Harmony whinnies shrilly up and down the arena, tail in the air as she races around. It takes Tristan a couple of minutes to catch her. I stand up and brush myself off. He brings the horse back over to me.

As if yesterday hadn't been bad enough! Now this. Tristan hands me the reins. "You okay?" he asks.

I nod and mutter, "Thank you."

"Happens to everyone," he says.

"Yeah. I need to get back on."

"Can I help? I can maybe coach a little. It's hard when you get a new horse. I totally get it. You should have seen Sebastian the first couple of months I had him."

"No," I reply, probably a little too curtly. "I've got this."

"Yeah, she's got it."

I hear Lydia from across the arena. Where had she come from? Where is the nearest rock, so I can quickly crawl under it?

Tristan looks back at her. "I'm just trying to help."

"She doesn't need your help. She said so, T."

He looks at me again. "I'm sorry. You're really okay?"

"I'm fine," I snap. "I think you better head off with Barbie."

He makes a funny face at me.

"Wait. I'm sorry." I pause for a moment. "Actually, can you give me a leg up? I don't want her to think that she can get away with that. I mean Harmony, of course."

"Sure." Tristan gives me a three-count and then hoists me back into the saddle. Harmony jigs to the side, but this time I'm prepared.

Lydia begins to clap haphazardly. "Nice going, *Scholarship.*"

"Screw you," I mutter as I bite back the tears that want really hard to come. I refuse to cry. I even ask myself, Why in the hell am I wanting to cry—because I came off? Because that stupid bitch saw the incident and made fun of me? Or because her gorgeous boyfriend, who I want to hate, has helped me and Harmony?

As I ride Harmony for about another twenty minutes, she settles back down and does as I ask, but neither of us is really happy.

When I take Harmony back to the barn, I'm still so upset that I'm afraid I might burst into tears. When I put Harmony away, she never gives me a damn word, a damn picture, a feeling. Nothing.

What is it with this mare? Or is it me?

I tuck my pride away and go back to my room where, alone, I bury my head in the pillow and bawl like a baby for the second time in two days. I want to go home and be with my Dean. With my mom. With Cole. With my friends and Gail. Back to all of it. And away from here. This is the worst feeling I've ever felt, because I am beginning to really dislike a horse for the first time in my life.

CHAPTER *eleven*

Luckily, Martina comes back cheerful and ready to go to the mixer. And I think my cry-athon actually did me some good, so I don't tell her what happened at the barn. Besides, we agreed to go, and Kayla has actually left us a message on our phone voice mail saying that we "really need to be there."

I do what I can to look decently mixer-able, but after spending half a day crying, I am puffy and red-eyed, so it's not easy.

Martina gives me a quick, curious look. "Viv, have you been crying?"

"Oh, no. I just have these stupid allergies." I am not good at lying and I think she knows this, but she doesn't press the issue, and I am grateful for that.

Mom and I went into Portland last week and she bought me some nice things—including this flouncy turquoise leopard-print skirt, which is much shorter than I am used to. Can I really wear this out in public?

I mean, I have spent the last ten years in either a pair of breeches or jeans, and a T-shirt or sweat shirt. But after I put on a little makeup on and curl my hair, I think I look okay—except for my legs, my ghostly, ghastly white legs.

"You look cute," Martina says. "I love your hair down."

"Thanks, but take a look at my chalk-stick legs."

Martina takes a step back. "Hmm. I see what you mean."

"Ouch! But true, right?"

"Wait. Don't worry—" She holds up a hand. "I have just what you need. Come—to the bathroom!" she orders.

I follow her and she holds up a spray can with the word "Luminosity" in gold letters. "What's that?"

"Instant self-tanner."

"Can't you get cancer from that stuff?" I ask.

"No, silly, that's tanning beds. This is going to be so easy. I'll just spray it on your legs and you'll get this nice golden glow."

"I'm not sure."

"My mom uses it all the time. Turn around."

With trepidation I do as ordered. The next thing I know, she is spraying the back of my legs. Then the front, and you know what? The stuff does take the chalky edge off!

"Told you," Martina says.

"I guess you did. Thanks. Shall we mix?"

"We shall," she replies. "And don't worry, I've got your back."

"And I've got yours."


Down in the main hall the mixer is already under way and my stomach is growing ever queasier. But, my mom is always telling me to "put myself out there," and that "good things happen when we least expect it." Mom, she loves a good cliché.

Inside, the place is really nice, all decorated in the school colors of silver and royal blue. There are tables with floral arrangements on them, and candles. I feel like I'm at a fancy wedding, not some high-school social. It's all a little surreal, and not half bad at all. I am used to going to high school dances where tissue streamers are all the decor, never candles or flowers.

Rihanna's latest is booming through the speakers and I immediately spot Tristan standing next to Lydia in the buffet line. That queasy feeling intensifies.

"Should we grab a bite?" Martina asks.

"Sure."

About the time Martina and I have nearly made it through the buffet line, Nate Deacon butts in between us. "Hey, girls. Don't mind if I sandwich in here, do you?"

"Actually yes," Martina replies.

"Ah, you are always such a buzzkill." He turns to me, and gives me a once-over. "You look great, Vivienne."

"Thanks," I mutter.

"You still got my number, right?" he asks.

"Oh, definitely."

"Hey, Nate, go troll somewhere else," Martina says.

He laughs. "Call me!"

"Jerk," I say.

"Yep. Come on, let's sit down."

Martina and I have just set our plates down at a table in the back corner when we are immediately joined by three other girls. I've already met the charming Emily Davenport.

I notice Martina frowning. "Hello."

"Hey, Tina," one of the girls says. She has long, dark hair that she keeping flipping back behind her shoulders.

"It's Martina."

"Oh right. So, *Martina*, aren't you going to introduce us to your friend?"

"Oh, let me," Emily says. "We met yesterday. Vivienne Taylor, these are my friends Alicia Vicenzia"—she points to the dark-haired girl—"and this is Shannon Burton. Shannon received the scholarship two years ago."

Shannon is petite, with brown hair and blue eyes. "I heard about you being bucked off."

There is this thing that happens to me when I am angry, embarrassed, or faced with confrontation—my ears heat up, and I know for a fact they first turn pink, then red, and finally violet. I think they have gone straight to violet.

"You know, I don't think I've ever been bucked off," Shannon says. "I hope you're *okay*."

Her fiendish pals all nod in mock sympathy.

"I'm completely *okay*. Thank you so very much."

"Cute skirt," Alicia says. "Very . . . what is it, Versace?"

"That's so funny," Emily chimes in. "Versace!"

Riley Reed takes the last empty chair at the table. "What's going on, ladies?"

"Ri—" Shannon smiles. "It's about time. We were just getting to know the new girl. This is Vivienne."

"We've met," Riley says. "And if I know you three, you aren't here to be the welcoming committee. You're here to be the bitches r' us committee."

"Riley," Alicia snaps. "Why would you say that?"

He rolls his eyes and tosses up his hands. "Oh my God, I have no idea why."

"You know, I think I've lost my appetite," I say to Martina.

"No, stay," Riley says, placing a hand over mine. "Seriously." He then looks at the girls. "Take your tired old mean-girls thing and go somewhere else. Don't you have lips to gloss or nails to paint, or someone else you can talk crap about?"

"Riley!" Shannon says.

"What?"

"Why are you acting like that? Like we aren't *friends*, and like you actually care about *her*?"

He leans back, tipping his chair onto two legs. "Maybe because I've decided that I am sick of all of you."

I can't believe this is happening! They all stand up and then Alicia bends down close to Riley, and I hear her say, "You'll be sorry for this, Riley. I have no clue what you're up to, but I think you've lost your mind." She then looks at me. "Nice self-tanner."

"No. I actually think I found it," he replies. "My mind, that is."

As they walk away, Martina looks as dumb-and-stunned as I must. But Riley is grinning hugely.

"Why did you do that?" I ask.

"Because it's true. I'm over their drama. But more important, in case you haven't noticed, I'm pretty sure you could use another friend around here."

CHAPTER *twelve*

bandonment, confusion, deep-hearted soulless-
ness, I felt all of that over the following week at
Fairmont. It was the same exact feeling that had
taken hold of me when my dad left us. But just like when he took
off . . . eventually life creeps back in, it envelops the bones and the
brain, and then encompasses the heart. Life must go on. There is no
way around that.

I have figured out in my years on this planet that I can choose
to let the crap eat away at me and keep me in that dark mixed-up
state, or I can just move the hell forward. Harmony may not want
to allow me into her world—even after nearly two weeks of grooming, riding, feeding, and attempts to bribe her with carrots or any
other treat that might appease, the mare still wants no part of me.
Fortunately, she hasn't pulled any more nasty stunts and is fairly
calm with me while I'm in the saddle.

Plenty of other horses want a part of me, though. I learned early on with my gift that as soon as horses figured out how well I understand them, then they usually share away.

The hardest thing is that I have no one to talk to about all of this. The only one who understands is Mom. But spilling about the more awful elements of life at Fairmont after how hard she worked to get me into this place? This is not an option. Instead, I keep our conversations light and just tell her what I know she wants to hear—mainly that I am having a great time and learning a ton. And I *am* learning a lot, and there are moments that are thrilling and fulfilling. Like when Newman Becker offered me accolades—and I quickly learned that he is not one to dole these out. Or, when Holden Fairmont—another one who is not easy to please—praised me.

As far as my regular classes go, they aren't easy, but I am enjoying the challenge. On the social front, I have made two fantastic friends—Riley and Martina—plus some friendly acquaintances. Sadly, Nate Deacon is in my barn management class. Sir Slimeball is always giving me these little looks and slightly dirty comments. I feel like he's up to something that has something to do with me. Paranoid much?

And the other Distracting Guy in that class? *Tristan.* He is on my mind way too much. *Ugh.*

Even my subconscious knows this. For the past few nights I have been having the same dream—sort of a nightmare, really. In it is a spotlight focused on a ladder in the dark. The ladder falls over and over again. I don't ever see it hit the ground. Everything goes dark before that. But when I wake up, I feel like *I* have repeatedly hit the ground. I've thought about this dream. A lot. Does it mean that I am in such foreign territory that it is like falling off a ladder over and over again?

My phone suddenly trills, breaking into my thoughts.

"Hi, Shnoopy!"

"Hi, Mom."

"So, how's the new horse?" Mom asks.

"She's good," I lie. I look over at Martina studying at her desk. We are going to dinner soon.

"Good? That's all you can say about her?"

"Yeah."

"Vivvie?"

"What, Mom?"

"I know you, and I know how you *relate* to horses. And I've never heard such a short answer from you regarding a horse, especially one who is now basically yours. When we talk, you barely mention her. She must have something to say to you. We both know they aren't short on opinions."

"True, but . . . this one kind of is. I guess you could say that she lives in the moment."

"Interesting."

"How's Dean?"

"He's *good*. Ren loves him and he seems to be getting on with her quite well, but I'm sure he misses you, like they all do. Like all of us do. But I want to hear more about this horse. Is she a good mover? Does she have the heart to event? What is she like in the dressage arena?"

"She's . . . great, Mom. Really. That's all I can say for now. Martina and I are getting ready to go to the cafeteria, and I have a ton of homework, so I want to grab some dinner and get to it."

"Of course. Have a good one, Shnoopy. Miss you. Love you. Wish I could be there this weekend."

"Me, too, Mom. Love you." I hang up the phone, and that miserable angst sets in again. My mom is not dumb. I know she could hear in my voice that things aren't as great as I keep insisting. Fact is, Harmony isn't giving me much on an emotional level. That's not to say that she isn't talented. Harmony can jump a four-foot oxer without an issue. She floats across the diagonal line in our dressage lessons like no other horse I have ever been on. We have not been out on the cross-country course yet, as course lessons are less frequent than dressage and show jumping. But if what I have learned about her athletic abilities already is indicative of what she can do out on course, then I have a strong sense that Harmony is going to shine out there as well.

But this issue of disconnect for me is huge. I can't deny it, and there is no one to talk to about it. Not Mom, who would know how the horse's lack of interest in connecting with me would affect me. Certainly no one at school would or could understand. I'm not going to be with the popular crowd. And if my gift is discovered, I am pretty sure that instead of people being in awe, it will only fuel the gossip pipeline. No, thank you.

I am also pretty sure that Riley's friendliness toward me has sealed my fate with what I have come to refer to as the drama zone, and shortened to "DZ."

"Everything okay back home?" Martina asks.

"Yeah. My mom, she just worries. You know how it is."

Martina closes her textbook. "I know, even with my parents living so close, they still worry like crazy."

"Uh-huh. Hey, can I ask you something that I've been wondering about?"

"Sure. But let's start walking. I told Riley we'd be there in five." She puts on some lip gloss.

I take a cursory look in the mirror attached to my dresser and sigh. I pull my hair back into a ponytail. "I was wondering, since your family is close by and all, why do you live on campus?"

"Well, my parents travel a lot. But I'm not a trust-fund brat. Those kids, it's just easier for their parents to toss money at them than to have them at home. For my parents, my dad is a movie producer and my mom"—she is blushing.—"is an actress. See, they just feel that because of my commitment to my horse, Fairmont is the best place for me. They don't have to worry about me here, and when they're home, I always visit on the weekends. In fact, you should come with me this weekend. My mom is going to be home from her location shoot in Sweden and my dad is in town, too. Thought I'd go up on Friday night. But wait, it's parents' weekend. Is your mom coming?"

"Not this time. She can't. The flight is expensive. Maybe I'll go up with you, but I kind of wanted to ride Harmony outside of a lesson. We seem to be having a hard time connecting." I had planned to take Harmony on a trail ride. I thought it might be a good chance to see if the mare and I might bridge the gap between us by going out on our own for a bit.

"I'm only going up Friday evening for dinner. My parents are great, and they love when I bring friends home."

"Okay then. Sure. Thanks."

Why am I being standoffish with her and Riley? Got to let my guard down. I realize this, I really do. But it's not easy. "Can I ask who your mom is?"

She blushes more deeply. "Erika Martín."

"Oh my God! Erika Martín! She is so beautiful and an amazing actress. I loved her in *A Time to Despair* when she kills the bad guy! She's your mom? I can't believe it!" I look at Martina's face. I frown. "Sorry. This probably the exact opposite of how you want people to act around you."

Martina nods but with a smile. "It's okay, really. I just don't like to make a big deal out of it. That's why I waited to tell you. I've had my share of grief around here because of who my parents are."

"What do you mean?" I ask, as we enter the cafeteria.

Martina gives me a head nod toward the DZ.

"Let me guess . . . jealousy issue?"

"Something like that." Martina waves at Riley, who is already waiting at our usual table.

I can't help but take note of the watchful eyes of the DZ turning to look our way. It's a quartet of frosty glares—Alicia, Shannon, Lydia, and Emily. The guys in the DZ are less involved in the drama. Except Nate Deacon, who is always ass-grabbing the girls in the DZ and then winking at me. Oh yeah. That just totally turns me on. That guy is such a tool. I have taken the tack of ignoring him. Hasn't seemed to faze him one bit. He wiggles his fingers at me in a slight wave.

I start to turn away from the DZ table, and I see that not only are the girls and Nate watching us, but so is Tristan. Only he isn't glaring. There is something else in his eyes, and I feel a rush go through me.

Martina is sure that Riley has a thing for me, although he hasn't abandoned his position as Shannon's "go-to guy" to join our little threesome. Riley is obviously super good-looking, and a ton of girls at the school want to go out with him. He has now been nothing but nice to me, but I just don't feel it. To be honest, I don't feel it from Riley either, despite Martina's insistence of his crush on me. Granted, when Austen kissed me at my going-away party, that threw me for a loop, too, but we had been flirting back and forth since the eighth grade, so I can sort of wrap my brain around that. But not *Riley*. It just doesn't ring true for me.

Then there's Tristan. Since he found me in Harmony's stall passed out, I have been having a tough time getting him out of my mind. I want to. Trust me. I really do. The last thing I need or want is a boyfriend. Guys bring trouble. Relationships cause problems and interfere with goals and hopes and dreams. I know this from experience. I was there as a ten-year-old to pick Mom up after Lane left us. Just left . . .

I know I will have to deal with my so-called father. He runs in equestrian circles on the East Coast, and if I continue to pursue my goals, Lane and I will eventually have a face-to-face. But for now, I just cannot *afford* to let him, or any guy, get in my way. Including Tristan.

Besides, who am I kidding? Tristan has no interest in me, probably nothing but pity for the new girl that his obnoxious girlfriend enjoys giving a hard time. He hasn't really said much to me since he found me that day on the ground. He's in my barn management class, which I think is interesting because it requires a lot of work, and most everyone knows that big money does not come from managing a barn. People usually do it because they truly love the horses and hard work. So I have to admit that Tristan's interest in the course has made me wonder a little more deeply about him. Or is he like Nate Deacon, who had no choice because he hadn't been able to get his first option in an extracurricular class?

Martina and I go through the line opting for our usual salad—then I add a bowl of mac and cheese. We make our way to Riley and sit down.

"My ladies," Riley says in a silly, deep voice. "About time you bitches arrived."

"Hey, pimp daddy." Martina giggles.

He smiles. "You guys look over our history project? I suck at those kind of projects. This school is so big on team crap. I hate it."

"Oh come on, Ri. It won't be that hard," I say. "Why don't the three of us do it together? Mr. Howard said we had that option."

"I know, but don't you think the team choice is harder?" Martina comments.

Our history teacher, Mr. Howard, has given us our first major assignment for the quarter. We can choose an event in history that could not have occurred or would not have happened as it had without horses. We then have to present the project as a film piece or something art-related that we put together with both an oral and written report—or it could be as if we were presenting the news on TV. I kind of think it sounds cool. Never in a million years would a project like this have been assigned at my old high school.

The other option is to take the individual choice and do the complete history of the horse, and present it in report form with visual aids. I think that sounds kind of boring, and also kind of easy to half-ass it. I like a challenge.

"Think of it. We could do some kind of documentary. The three of us could look into different areas and present it. What if we did something about the Olympics and the history of horses in the Olympics? We could interview Newman Becker. I mean, he's right here on campus, and don't we all have that one goal in common?" I ask.

"What goal?" Riley replies.

"To go to the Olympics? Isn't that why we're here?"

"Not all of us," Martina says.

Riley shakes his head. "I like riding and I love my horse, but I can't say that's my ultimate goal."

"It's not really mine either," Martina says. "I'm here to learn all that I can about horses and riding, but eventually I want to go into film like my parents. For now, this is what I love, though."

"Okay. It seems I'm a lonely minnow in the big ocean of ambition."

They laugh.

"But if you really want to go into film, Martina, isn't this a good idea?" I ask.

"It sounds hard, though."

"We're here because it's supposed to be easy?"

"Ah, you are a smart one, Vivvie. One of the three dozen things I like about you." Riley winks at me.

My stomach knots. I can't deny the guy's cuteness factor, but all I want is a friend. I swear. "Good. So, you guys are in?"

We all toast to our project.

"You know, you aren't the only one who has Olympic dreams," Riley says.

"Oh yeah?"

"Lydia does, too."

And as if the DZ queen has telepathy, she is, at that moment, in earshot of our table, getting a refill on her diet soda. She flips around and saunters over. "My name is being uttered among you. Why?"

"I was just telling Vivienne here that like her, you have the goal of the gold," Riley says.

Lydia pauses before saying anything and pointedly looks at my dinner. "I'm not too worried about competition from Scholarship." My name for her little group, the DZ, has not fallen on deaf ears; they in turn pinned me with the name Scholarship.

"Not now, or in the future," she continues. "It's obvious that you won't be able to stay fit enough to compete at high levels. I mean, come on, Vivienne—macaroni and cheese? Keep eating like that, and there won't be a horse who will want to pack your fat ass around."

Riley places a hand over mine and Martina grabs the other, probably figuring that I am about ready to stand up and shove Lydia's face into the pasta.

"Lydia, don't worry about my diet," I say. "What *you should* worry about is our first event. It's in what? Two weeks? Then we'll see who winds up with a blue and who might actually have the potential to go all the way."

She turns on her heels and heads back to her zone, where she immediately begins planning my demise, I'm sure.

"Nice comeback, Vivvie!" Martina says.

"Thanks." I force a smile. The thing is that as much of a bitch as Lydia Gallagher is, I've watched the girl ride—she can ride. She has a talented horse, and *she* also has talent. I look down at my high-calorie meal and pray that the words I just threatened my nemesis with aren't ones that I will be eating.

# RILEY

## CHAPTER *thirteen*

Riley has decided to do something bold to make it clear that he isn't returning into Shannon's arms, or to what Vivvie has coined the DZ. He loves that she's done that and finds it amusing. He knows Lydia and her sidekicks are not happy with him, but Shannon is still attempting to hook him back.

He likes Vivienne Taylor and her smart mouth. He likes that she doesn't let Lydia and her group get to her. In all honesty, he likes Vivvie. She isn't pushy or clingy. She's smart and sweet, and like him, she is at Fairmont for what seem to be the right reasons.

He is there to learn, too, but he also knows deep inside that his reasons might not be as noble as Vivvie's. Riley has a real need to escape his family. He can't take his father's sermons and lectures. His parents are unrealistic and judgmental—strict and condescending. He plays nice and he plays along, but when he's at home for breaks, all he wants to do is get back to Fairmont.

His father, in particular, is intimidating and difficult. Riley had been shocked when they agreed to allow him to attend Fairmont. But the few thousand miles that separated Riley and his family in Virginia was still not enough. Riley is already making plans for after graduation. He knows he'll be cut off from his family's money once he put his plans into fruition, but he also knows that if he doesn't take the risk, he'll never get out from under their heavy thumb.

As they leave the cafeteria, Riley touches Vivienne's shoulder. "Um, can you walk with me? I want to ask you something." He smiles at Martina.

"You guys go on. I have to get back and finish my Spanish homework. We can get started on our project later."

"Sounds good," Riley replies. "Vivienne?"

"Yeah. Great. Okay. I have a lot of homework too, but sure I can walk with you. Where are we going?"

"Why don't we go see our horses?" Riley asks. He's nervous, and he really hopes that what he wants to ask Vivienne won't ruin anything between them. Like everything in his life, Riley needs to play this close to the vest, and hope he can keep it all together. "It's so nice out here," he says.

"It is," Vivienne replies.

"You like it here?" he asks.

"The DZ keeps their cauldron stirring, but other than that, what's not to like? It's beautiful. The classes are interesting. The horses are amazing. It's a big adjustment, though. I'm not used to all of this, uh . . . wealth."

"It can be overwhelming. I suspect that being the kid on scholarship brings an extra layer of pressure."

"It does. But how about you? Why did you decide to come to Fairmont? I can't believe I just assumed everyone here wants to be an Olympian."

"Well, there are lots of kids here who have some pretty high expectations when it comes to their riding. But I doubt there are many who will get even close to making it to the Olympics, though." He stops and looks at her, takes in how her blue eyes sparkle. "But I think you will."

"Really?"

"I've been in the lessons with you. You are *that* good, and Lydia should be *that* scared."

"She's good, too."

"True. But I've seen some spectacular riding on your part. Harmony doesn't look terribly easy to ride. That's probably why Kayla paired you with her. She knew you could handle her. As far as Lydia goes, I think in anything in life, you only get so far on talent. Attitude and drive matters about as much. You have the total package, Vivvie."

"And you are good with the compliments, Riley Reed. So, you know what I want from this place, but you still haven't told me why you're here."

He does something in that moment that he has learned to do, and do quite well. He hates doing it to Vivienne, who he cares for, but does it anyway. He lies. "I'd like to train horses. Yeah. I want my own facility and business some day. I love being around them. So . . . it's what I want to do."

The lie isn't about his affinity for horses but about his reasons for being at Fairmont. Vivvie chose to come to Fairmont. Riley escaped to it. Through the last few years, he has discovered that he has no other choice.

CHAPTER *fourteen*

I'm a little confused by what Riley wants to ask me. It's good getting to know a little more about him, but I am still curious. I have the sense neither one of us is ready to bring it up. We continue to the barns as our conversation about him wanting to become a trainer drifts into silence.

In the back of my mind I can't help thinking that, in a few moments, I will again come face-to-face with a horse who feels nothing for me. If I were at home, visiting Dean before doing homework would be the highlight of my evening.

We walk past the lake, where a dozen ducks maneuver through soft ripples of water. In the darkening fall sky, the ripples of water makes it look as though there are thousands of coins shimmering in the reflection caused by the descending sun. Pepper and willow trees sway gracefully along the bank as the ocean breeze shifts through their leaves. The grounds at Fairmont continue to amaze me.

"What did you want to talk to me about?" I finally ask, breaking the silence and the growing tension between us.

He sighs. "I don't know why this is so hard."

"What's so hard?" I ask.

"Oh God. Will you go to the Homecoming Dance with me?" he spits out.

*Damn! What to say?* We keep walking. I am stunned. We turn the corner into the barn breezeway. "Ri, we are *friends*."

"I know." He starting to say something else when we spot Tristan and Lydia. They're between Harmony and Sebastian's stalls, and neither one looks pleased.

"Come on," Lydia says. "Why not there? It'll be so romantic. I thought you wanted me to be happy."

Tristan spots us and immediately takes Lydia's hand. "Come on. Let's go talk about this somewhere else." He nods at Riley. "Hey, man. Hi, Vivienne."

Lydia shoots her trademark scowl at me. I hear her say as they walk away, "Wonder what is up with those two? From Shannon to *that*. God."

I close my eyes for a second.

"Forget her," Riley says. "We both know what she is. And I like you. You're pretty. You're smart and sweet. Plus, you are real."

"Riley, I don't want a boyfriend. I'm not here for any of that. I can't let anything or anyone get in the way of my goals."

"I don't want a girlfriend."

I stop and look at him. "I am also not into the whole friends-with-benefits type of thing."

"Me neither. I wasn't even thinking it. Honest."

"Let me get this straight. You think I'm pretty. You *like* me, but like *me*, you don't want a relationship. And this isn't about sex. You just want to be my friend and have me go to the dance with you."

Now he's openly grinning. "That's it. I have goals, too, Viv, and I think anything more than a friendship in my life right now would complicate everything for me. But I do like to dance."

"Okay then. But I kinda suck at dancing."

"I don't care. We are going to have a terrific, *friendly* time."

We reach Harmony's stall. Riley pulls a horse cookie from his pocket and hands it to me.

"She never seems interested in me or treats. Or in anything, really," I tell him. "She's responsive during lessons and hasn't made any stupid moves since our first outing together, but she's kind of—"

"Aloof?"

"Yeah. I think that's a good word for her. This might sound weird, but I think she must have really loved her former owner—Dr. Miller. She just doesn't want to attach to me."

"I don't think it sounds weird."

"You don't?"

"No. I think when an animal is attached, and then you're suddenly gone from their lives, they have feelings about it."

I've "talked" with enough horses to know this to be true. What I don't understand about this horse is that she doesn't tell me a damn thing, and I can't tell Riley how I know this. Instead I ask: "Did you know Dr. Miller?"

"I did. I came back early to attend her funeral. A lot of kids did."

"I take it then that she was liked by a lot of people."

"Loved, really. I mean the lady was super supportive of our school. She understood horses in a way that I've never seen before. We've all heard the term *horse whisperer*, and most people think it's kind of corny, but if there is such a thing, then I think Dr. Miller had the gift of complete empathy and communication with the horses she worked with."

*How to respond?* Horse whispering is a method of training that emerged through the study of how wild horses communicate with one another. It's not the same as the type of communication that I have with horses. But when Riley says the words *empathy* and *communication* together, it makes me wonder if Dr. Miller also had the gift. I can't be the only one, right?

"What else did you know about Dr. Miller?"

"Well, she was recently engaged and planning a wedding."

"That makes it even sadder. Who was she marrying?"

"A guy named Christian Albright, a friend of Holden and Kayla's. Dr. Miller was Holden's cousin. This guy is an event rider back East. He's a pretty big up-and-comer. I think that Harmony may have been sent out from his barn a year or so ago, when Dr. Miller moved up to prelim. She was a good rider, too. But her practice kept her from competing as much as I think she wanted to."

"I've heard of Christian Albright." Interesting to know that Harmony may have originally belonged to him. ´

"The guy was totally broken up at the funeral. I heard he's still in town helping store her things and getting the horses moved out that need to be sold. Harmony and another horse who had been hers were donated to the academy. But she also had a couple of quarter horses who wouldn't have fit the program here. Not sure what happened to them."

"There's another horse here who'd been Dr. Miller's?" I asked.

"Yeah. A gelding. He's actually up in Kayla and Holden's private barn. Kayla is riding him. Looks like a three-star horse, if you ask me, maybe even a four-star." He raises his eyebrows. "Like you, our director would love to be on an Olympic team."

"Really?" I know Kayla is an accomplished rider, and she's probably only in her mid-thirties, which for an Olympic equestrian is a pretty average age. I secretly want to one day be the youngest rider on the Olympic team. My mom has always told me there is no hurry, but there is something that burns within me and drives me toward my goals.

"I think she's been waiting for the right horse to come along. Two years ago, Dr. Miller had to put Kayla's horse down out on course. He got hung up coming out of the water and fractured his stifle. It was terrible."

"That is horrible on every front."

Riley nods. "It is. I think almost everyone here is hoping that this new horse works out for Kayla."

"He's up in the private barn. Hmmm."

"What?" Riley asks.

"I'd like to see him."

"Can't do it tonight. That barn is closed down, and security is ultra tight with the Fairmonts' horses. But Kayla rides him at dawn every morning. I've seen her out in both the dressage ring and the jump arena. They are great together. You should watch one day."

I have a thought—if Kayla's horse lived with Harmony at Dr. Miller's, then maybe Kayla's horse will communicate with me about what went on there. Maybe he will be able to tell me what in the hell is wrong with my shut-down mare.

# TRISTAN

## CHAPTER *fifteen*

Tristan is tossing and turning in his bed.

*How can I have been so stupid as to confide in her?*

What Lydia knows could ruin his family and his future. And walking on a tightrope around her is getting exhausting.

Then there's Vivienne Taylor, though he can tell she has no interest in him. God, she is beautiful. But Riley and her seem to have an interest in each other. He wonders if Riley is a part of the scholarship-girl induction. Maybe his "liking" of Vivienne is more about the bet. Tristan hasn't asked Ri if he is in on it because he thinks it is so stupid. Nate Deacon is such an ass. He can't imagine Riley would be involved.

He has to give props to his roommate for making a strategic exit from Lydia and her crew. Then again, there's no a skeleton in Riley's closet holding him hostage. If he hadn't had two shots of tequila *that* night, and felt so scared about what he'd discovered that he felt he had to tell someone, then he, like Riley, could have ditched Lydia.

Most guys at the school would kill to get with Lydia Gallagher. Here's a girl who is totally into him, wants to sleep with him, but the fact is that she is a total bitch to everyone outside her world. He can't stop questioning what that says about him.

*Shit! I'm never gonna get some sleep.*

Tristan decides to get up, grab a bottle of water, maybe look out the window at the waves crashing down onto the sandy beach. He feels like a crashing wave himself. Oh, to have a TV in the room at moments like these.

Riley walks in a few minutes later. "Sorry, bro, didn't mean to wake you."

"You didn't. I was awake anyway. I was thinking about stuff."

"You? What's up?"

"Nothing."

"Right. Let me guess . . . Lydia?"

Tristan sighs. "Yeah."

"What's the problem?"

"This is Lydia we are talking about. She wants me to be this guy that I'm not."

Riley sticks out his chest and bats his eyelashes. "Oh, Tristan, why can't you fly me on your private jet to Hawaii where we can be all alone?"

"Pretty much."

"I guess it's all in deciding what you want." Riley grabs a bottle of water and sits at the table across from Tristan.

"What do you mean?"

Riley twists the cap off the water bottle and takes a long sip. "I like people with substance, man. Shannon Burton is hot and super sexy and all that shit, but that's about it."

"And Vivienne Taylor?"

"Vivienne is cool. She's what my uncle John would refer to as a classic beauty, but she's more than that. She's smart, she knows what she wants, she . . ."

"Has substance." Tristan finishes his sentence.

"Yeah."

"You know you're number *one*, and I'm *three*."

"Nate is two. I know. That's ridiculous. Vivvie isn't the kind of girl to fall for that anyway," Riley replies.

"So, you're not in?" Tristan asks, relieved.

"Hell no! Tell me you aren't either."

"No way, man. I can see you have a thing for her. That's cool."

Riley doesn't reply.

"Substance, huh? Vivienne Taylor. Yeah. I can see that." Tristan picks the conversation back up.

"Let's face it, none of the chicks you hang out with have much of that. You've got Lydia, who what, her parents laid out how much for that new horse out there? Over a hundred grand? I don't know about you, but the girl didn't seem to be all that upset when Haute was put down," Riley says. "Kind of cold. Not much substance there."

Riley was referring to last year when Lydia's fancy jumper, Haute Couture, got sick and died from kidney failure. Dr. Miller euthanized her, and Newman Becker personally helped Lydia and her family find a new horse over the summer. Tristan knew that if Newman helped get Lydia a new horse, her folks had dropped some serious cash on it.

"No. I think she was honestly upset about that," Tristan says, remembering how he had hooked up with Lydia at about the time her mare had to be put down. In fact, she had cried on his shoulder and he'd comforted her.

"Yeah, well, all I can say is if you had to put my horse down like that, I wouldn't be bouncing back here all gloating over my shiny new one."

"You're sounding as judgmental as she does." Tristan squirts water from his bottle at Riley. They both start laughing. "Seriously though," Tristan says. "What should I do? Should I be the ass who hooks up all the way with Lydia because I can?"

"You are asking a guy who, believe it or not, still believes in true love and all that shit. And in *substance*. Wrong guy to ask, bro. You gotta make up your mind as to what your priorities are."

"C'mon, we are only seventeen," Tristan remarks.

"Right. But does that mean we have to be shallow? To party and take the easy road just because it's *easy*?"

"Shit, Ri, when did you get so philosophical? Were you ever a kid?"

"Yeah, I'm way deep. So what are you going to do?"

Tristan shrugs, then squirts Riley again.

"Tell you what, when you decide you want some substance, you know where we sit," Riley says. "Going to bed. I have buckets in barn three in the morning. Don't you have buckets, too?"

"Yeah, in my barn actually, tomorrow. Of course it seems to be the high-maintenance barn."

"Your horse is in it. What'd you expect?" Riley laughed. "Like rider, like horse."

"Yes. My horse has some issues."

"Don't we all," Riley replies. "Night, T. Don't think too hard on this stuff. You're a good guy. You'll figure it out."

Tristan sits back in the chair, finishing his water. One thing now seems clear—Riley and his girl of substance are forming something together. So pursuing her is out of the question. Isn't it?

CHAPTER *sixteen*

I wake up an hour earlier the next morning hoping to catch Kayla on her new horse. I had that stupid ladder dream again. It makes me feel as if I haven't had any real sleep. I shower and quickly pack up my books and riding attire for the day. Wednesdays are my busiest day, and I won't have time to come back and change before my afternoon dressage lesson with Holden. Our first few lessons haven't gone all that well. It wasn't Harmony, who did everything I'd asked. It was me. The other day, Holden took me aside afterward and said how it would take time for us to get into sync, being that we were new to each other. I'm doubtful that's all that there is to it, but I'm determined to figure her out.

Martina wakes up as I am halfway out the door.

"Where you going so early?" she asks.

"I thought I'd catch Kayla on her new horse. Riley told me she rides at dawn."

"Cool. Lunch?"

"I'll be there." I shut the door behind me and walk to the dressage arena, where I'm happy to spot Kayla on top of a near seventeen-hand mahogany bay, truly beautiful. As I approach he looks to me to possibly be a Westphalian. Definitely a warmblood.

There's Holden sitting inside the gazebo designated for the instructors. "Nice, nice," he says. "Move him up a little. There you go. Good. Good. Reach down and scratch his neck. Beautiful. Just beautiful work."

I stand off to the side, watching magic take place in front of me. Dressage is an art form. It perfectly defines the harmonic relationship between horse and rider. It's poetry in motion. Each movement needs to be executed just so, memorized by the rider and communicated to the animal. To witness grand prix dressage ridden with such grace and precision literally takes my breath away.

Kayla and this horse have the movements and rhythm down in a way that I can only dream of one day accomplishing.

"Vivienne!"

Holden is calling me over. "Come here. This is the best seat in the house."

I walk over. "Really? I can watch from here?"

"I invited you."

There is an unspoken rule that students are not allowed in instructors' boxes. "Thank you."

"You can learn a lot by watching from the ground."

I take a seat next to him. Like everyone else in this particular paradise, Holden Fairmont has movie-star good looks—like a younger, taller George Clooney. If my mom saw him, she'd probably turn bright red and fumble her words. I've noticed Lydia and the DZ minions drooling over Holden. Understandably.

"They are amazing together," I say.

"They are," he replies. I can hear the slight Canadian clip to his speech. "We finally have a horse who really connects with my wife. It is not a happy story how he came here, but it is what it is at this point."

"I heard," I admit. "I'm sorry for your loss. Dr. Miller was your cousin?"

"Yes. And she was a good woman. Moved to the States with us when I was ten. She actually lived with my family because her mom had some troubles." He doesn't elaborate.

"So Kayla's horse . . ."

"Timbre. We call him Timmy."

"Timmy. He's what? A Westphalian?"

Holden turns and looks at me, eyebrows raised. "Good girl. You know your breeds."

"My mom is a vet. I had access to every breed book, history, vet med, you name it. My house back home is filled with books."

He smiles. "You're going to do well here, Vivienne."

"I hope so."

"Is everything okay?"

"Well, it's hard socially. I've made a couple of good friends, but these kids are a tough crowd."

"I don't doubt it," he replies. "But your talent is why you're here. You'll be fine socially. I'm sure of that."

"I'm not so sure about my 'talent' at this point, either."

He smiles sympathetically. "You grew up with horses. You should know it isn't always an easy thing. The mare has had some trauma, and the atmosphere is much more intense here than at my cousin's place."

Timmy and Kayla come over to the side of the arena. "Hey," Kayla says breathlessly.

"Hi. I came to watch you ride."

"What did you think?"

"I think you two are phenomenal. I wish I could ride like you."

"You will." She smiles widely.

"Can I pet him?"

"Sure."

I step over the rail. In the cool morning, I can see the horse's breath as he blows it out rapidly, coming down from the workout. I place a hand on his sweaty neck, where his veins are popping against his coat. He's absolutely gorgeous. I look up into his large eyes and envision Harmony in my mind.

It works! He shows me an image of the mare, a woman, and a heart. It means there was a deep love between Harmony and Dr. Miller. Next, he shows me darkness—a darkness that means something. I show him Harmony again.

And then he shows me a ladder. The same ladder I have been dreaming about for the past week.

"Hey, Vivienne, I need to go this afternoon after lessons and pick up Harmony and Timmy's winter blankets from their old home. Would you want to go with me?" Kayla asks. "I know you haven't seen much of California, and it's a nice drive to Serena's, plus we can touch base on how things are going for you so far. We could even have dinner on the way back."

I am too stunned to respond. That ladder, it means something.

"Vivienne? Would you like to go with me?"

"Sure. Sounds good."

"All right, me and this guy better get back to work, and you have just enough time to get some breakfast and get to class."

"See you later!"

I walk numbly to the cafeteria for a bagel and a coffee, still totally distracted.

Darkness. Harmony. The ladder?

I drink my coffee and walk to class completely consumed by this mystery.

CHAPTER *seventeen*

ig sigh walking into barn management class—
a heaviness weighing on my shoulders. I cannot
chase out of my head the image of the ladder and
what it might possibly mean.

It's my first period, and although I love it because I have an
interest in one day running my own private facility, there is always
*that* distraction.

Two rows behind me to the left.

Tristan Goode.

He comes in five minutes late to class. My stomach completely
zigzags when he walks on by, and this pisses me off. I tilt my head
to the side, steal a glance. Why does he have to look so good? With
his short sandy hair that has the slightest of waves to it. Then there
are his green eyes. Oh my God. They are like this kind of olive
green with gold flecks, and thick dark lashes framing them. Usually
things like long eyelashes don't matter much to me. But I want to
touch Tristan's lashes. I hate myself for this.

And his lips. Do not get me started. Thick and full, and perfectly shaped. His body is genius. I am sorry, but Tristan Goode has a body I can only compare to Michelangelo's Statue of David—sans the . . . that one part. I've only seen the guy clothed, and that is the only way I will ever see him.

I really want to hate him as much as I hate myself for obsessing over him. Tristan Goode takes up way too much space in my head.

I turn back to face Mr. Bromley, who wears an unamused look as he watches the latecomer set his books down. "Mr. Goode, do you have a problem getting to class on time? And you need to take off the baseball cap. You know the rules about hats in class."

I so want to turn around to see his face, but I don't. A few kids do, but not me.

"No, sir. I'm sorry. I had buckets to do in Barn Seven this morning, and I had a slight incident with one of the horses."

"Slight incident? Expand, please?"

I hear him sigh. "Vivienne's horse . . ."

I turn around.

Nate Deacon sits directly behind me and flashes me his smarmy smile. I roll my eyes at him and stare at Tristan.

"Vivienne's horse, Harmony, she pretty much kicked at me and knocked the bucket out of my hand, spilling it all over." He's putting his baseball cap into his backpack and then looks up, catching my eye.

A few kids giggle.

"She didn't kick you, did she?" Mr. Bromley asks.

I can't say a word. If it had been Dean, I would have immediately come to his defense, suggesting Tristan might have done something stupid. But with Harmony, I have a feeling it was she who had done something stupid, and I feel miserable. Kicking is simply one of those things that can't be tolerated from a horse. If it turns into a habit, Harmony will be removed from the program. Maybe that would be the best thing for all. I can't believe I'm thinking this way.

I was not raised to be a quitter, and here I am considering quitting on an animal who's had a tough few weeks. No. I have to get through to her.

Tristan looks at me again. "You may want to watch her, Vivienne. I think she has a nasty streak."

All I can do is nod.

"Personally, I like a little bit of nasty." This is from Nate. *Such a tool.* Can someone please get me out of here?

"Did you report the incident to either one of the Fairmonts?"

"Not yet. I knew I was already late to class, and I thought I should speak with Vivienne first about it."

"Well, that's thoughtful," Mr. Bromley replies, "But per the rules you need to report this. I suggest doing so right after class."

I slink down in my chair and try hard to turn my focus onto Mr. Bromley's lecture on managing finances when running a barn. But pretty much the next hour is spent inside my head, racking my brain over Harmony and feeling bad that she kicked out at Tristan. I know I should talk to him about her after class but . . . oh God! I feel sick to my stomach.

As class comes to a close, Mr. Bromley finally catches my attention. "Your quarter assignment will be working with another member in class. One of you will be working from the trainer point of view at a barn. That means you manage the horses, help bring in the clients, keep track of all things associated with your training, employees, that sort of thing. The other one of the team will be the owner/barn manager. Your job will be to manage the finances over-all and keep things within a budget, as well as promote the barn and communicate well with the trainer. This incorporates econom-ics, marketing, and business. It's all in the syllabus I am passing out. If you have questions, we can go over it tomorrow. Grading will be on the quality of the overall project, individual work, and how you work as a team. We all know in the equestrian business, as with most things in life, there is a need for a team mentality. Good!" He claps his hands together. "Okay, we have twelve in this class, so that makes it perfect for the two-person teams. I am going to number one through six. Find your corresponding number and there's your team partner."

Mr. Bromley gets to the end of my row and I'm number six. My stomach begins sinking rapidly as I calculate as quickly as I can who will also be number six. My brain reaches the answer as Mr. Bromley says it aloud. "Mr. Goode, you are number six."

TRISTAN

CHAPTER *eighteen*

As Vivienne walks quickly down the hall, Tristan tries to catch up with her. When she finally reaches her locker and she's twisting her combination lock, he says, "Hi."

"Hi." she says, not altogether looking at him.

He notices that she's having difficulty getting the lock undone. "I thought maybe we should talk about Harmony."

She gets her locker open, puts away a few books, grabs some new ones. "I'm sorry she kicked you."

"Yeah, no worries. I just . . ."

Vivienne closes her locker and faces him. "Just what?"

He thinks: *Man, she has pretty blue eyes.* "I'm not going to report what she did. She was just being a horse, and maybe feeling uh, full of herself. Maybe she's in season?"

Oh God, how ridiculous does that sound? Tristan wants to bang his head against her locker.

"Yes, because all females *in season* want to kick the crap out of anything male?" This earns a small smile from Tristan.

"Seriously, I wouldn't want you to get into trouble on either Harmony or my account."

"Oh, no worries. Hey, we should maybe figure out when we can get together and work on the barn management project. It's pretty intense."

She looks away before answering. "Yeah. Let's do that."

"What day?" he asks.

She leans back against her locker. "I think Wednesdays. I can meet with you on Wednesdays."

He places a hand on the locker next to her and leans in slightly—close enough that he can smell her perfume. Or is it just her? *Mmm.* Either way, he finds it . . . intoxicating. "Good. Library?"

"Yes," she says in a barely audible voice.

*Is she nervous?*

"Five thirty? Maybe for an hour, so then we can head out for dinner," he says.

"What would your girlfriend say about that?"

"I didn't mean . . . I meant we could work on our project for an hour, and then you can go have your dinner and I'll have mine. I assume that you and Riley like to eat together."

"What do you mean about Riley and me?"

He notices her ears turning red, and he wants to laugh because it's kind of cute. She's been playing tough girl, and now he has her. He would *love* to have dinner with her. He would really love that. "You and Riley? You are going out, right?"

"No. He's my friend."

"Oh. I just thought, because you guys spend a lot of time together and he talks about you all the time. You know he's my roommate, right?"

She shifts uncomfortably. "I have to go."

"Right. See you in class and next Wednesday at the library." Tristan watches her walk away. The way he caught her looking at him has not been lost on him at all. And now, to learn that she and Riley are not going out—now that *is* interesting. Does it change anything for him? Probably not. First off, he knew that his buddy had a thing for her. It was so obvious from the *substance* talk.

Secondly, there is Lydia.

He's started to walk toward his locker when Nate stops him. "Hey, man . . . saw you talking to Vivienne. So, you're in, huh? Nice you get to be her *partner*. That should make things a little easier for you. But I am still going to win this thing."

"I was talking to her about her horse, and I am *not* in. Just let it go, Nate."

"Let it go? No way. The pool is at two grand right now and climbing! Plus, I want into those panties."

"I seriously doubt that is going to happen," Tristan says.

"Oh, I got ways. Could be a fun little chase. You could get yourself a piece on the side. Not bad. I mean, I'm hanging out with Emily, you know, but that doesn't stop me from thinking that this Vivienne chick could be a party. And it's all between us . . . the boys. Come on, what do you say? Might make some money, and . . ."

"I said no."

Nate takes a step back and holds his hands up in the air. "Okay, bro. But if you change your mind, I think you got a lot of the boys swinging for Team Tristan."

Tristan feels an intense need to protect Vivienne. He respects her. Kids don't come to Fairmont on scholarship without working their asses off, and he doesn't want to see her chased away by jealous girls and idiotic guys. He begins walking to his next class. How can he protect this girl from all the BS at Fairmont? *Does she even want me to?* He's pretty sure that she doesn't. He can't do anything to save her without ruining his own future.

CHAPTER *nineteen*

My interesting day continues. Being paired with Tristan, then having that awkward conversation by my locker, still has me thrown. How in the world am I supposed to meet with this guy to work on our project on a regular basis? Come on! Oh God, did he notice my ears? I could feel them burning when he said that thing about Riley and me.

On the positive side, my dressage lesson is going well. Better than well, in fact. I really thought it was going to suck because today is a group lesson, and in my group are my BFFs—Lydia and Emily.

I tack up Harmony, not expecting any direct communication from her, but I still feel bad that I can't help her. At least we are becoming a fairly decent team in the riding arenas. Yes, she is a handful. I can always feel that nervous energy bubbling up from inside her, especially during our jump lessons. However, I am able to maintain that energy and keep her mind focused. So although she isn't talking to me, maybe she is listening to me?

We warm up our horses before Holden begins teaching. As much as I can't stand Lydia, she does have a presence on her mare, Geisha, who is a spectacular black Selle Français. I can see out of the corner of my eye, though, that Geisha is being difficult for Lydia. Kind of out of character for the horse.

Then there's Emily, who from my perspective never seems to really want to be on the back of a horse. She almost appears to despise it. She is a good rider, though.

As the lesson starts, Holden has to really work with Lydia and Geisha. "No, Lydia. Get your leg underneath you a little farther. Look at Vivienne."

Does he have to say that?

"Better. Now quit hanging on her. The more you pull on her mouth, the more she pulls back. Right? Who is going to win that battle?"

One of Holden's rules is that when he asks a question, he expects it to be answered. Even if the answer is, "I don't know."

"Miss Gallagher? Do you hear me?"

"Of course," she replies snottily.

"Okay, then, who is going to win the war if you constantly hang on her mouth?"

"Her!" she shoots back.

"Correct. What is the answer then? What should you do?"

She sighs and shrugs.

"Emily?" he asks.

She shrugs, too.

Oh boy, these two and their peas-in-a-pod mode. They know the answer. It's basic.

"Vivienne? What would you do?"

I feel framed. "I'd put my leg on, soften my elbows, and use my hips to rotate with her movements. As you said, the tenser you become, the tenser the horse becomes, and it is a battle the rider won't ever win."

"Correct! Girls, you are on thousand-pound animals. They will win the tug-of-war. Okay, back to work."

It is five minutes later and I see Lydia seesawing on her horse's mouth again.

Holden sees it, too. "Lydia! Get off her!"

"What? Why?"

"You know why. If you can't follow instructions, and then you get angry about it and take it out on her, then you don't ride for the rest of the day."

"I wasn't . . . ," she starts to protest.

"Off!" he says. "Emily can put your horse away. I don't need anyone who is in a belligerent and foul mood to be dealing with an animal. She doesn't deserve it. I also want you in my office at seven thirty tomorrow morning."

She swings her leg over and jumps off, handing him the reins. "Yes, sir," she replies.

The rest of the lesson is peaceful and nearly perfect.

When the lesson is over and we head back to the barns, I notice a woman approaching Emily. She is tall and dressed in riding attire herself. "Emily!" she calls out.

Holden has Lydia's horse. "Mrs. Davenport, it's nice to see you," he says.

"Hello, Mo-ther."

"Looks like my daughter has some work to do."

"*Mom*."

"She's doing rather well," Holden replied.

"I took some video today. I think we need to sit down and go over it," Mrs. Davenport says. "From where I was, it looks as if your new student has quite an edge over Emily."

"Mrs. Davenport, Emily is a fine rider, and she is improving every day."

"I have an opinion on that. Emily, you will be coming to dinner with me tonight, and we will review your performance."

I keep walking, not wanting to get caught up in any of that. I glance back, and Emily looks shattered. I feel kind of sorry for her.

What looks so pretty on the outside around Fairmont—the beautiful kids who seem to have perfect lives—now looks less so. In fact, I wonder if, like Emily, the kids she hangs out with are all living some big charade?

CHAPTER *twenty*

While I put Harmony away, I tell her, "I am going to your old home tonight, to get your winter blanket and turnout sheet." I wish I knew what her old home looked like, or even the color of her blanket, so that I could picture those for her.

"You were a really good girl today. Thank you. That Lydia was not so good, huh? Her poor horse."

And then . . . I get something! She shows me a kick to Lydia's butt. I start laughing and practically crying at the same time! "Yes, you're right! She does deserve a kick in the ass. Speaking of, why did you kick Tristan this morning?" I picture Tristan in my head.

She shows me a baseball cap. "A cap? What?"

Again, she shows me the cap. He had worn a cap in class. "I don't understand."

"Vivienne?"

I turn around to see Kayla. "Oh, hi."

"You about ready? I want to get on the road, so we aren't back too late."

"Let me just put her back in the stall." As I do this, I whisper, "I don't know what the cap means, but thank you for telling me about it."

I leave Harmony, elated that she has given me some tidbit. I want more.

Driving inland, Kayla tells me we are headed to an area called Tarzana. The traffic is light on the back roads. Along the way, we make small talk about school. I am still curious about why she invited me.

We pull into Dr. Miller's place about twenty minutes later. It's impressive. Not on the scale that Fairmont is, but still nice. We drive up a long driveway with rosebushes on either side. There is a shed row to the right of us, and on the left-hand side a riding arena, as well as a pretty ranch-style house at the end of the driveway. Kayla pulls around back. I see a few empty corrals and a round pen, and then a main barn in the far left corner. Lights are on inside the barn. A couple of cars are also parked nearby.

"Huh," Kayla says. "I figured Christian would be packing the rest of Serena's things up, but I didn't expect anyone else to be here."

"Christian is—was—Serena's fiancé. I suppose the other car might belong to a former boarder. Serena ran a rehab facility for injured horses," she explains. "And she also on occasion would bring some of her sick patients here for observation and help."

"Oh." I don't know what else to say. I want to ask her about Harmony and Christian Albright's place back East, but at this moment, I'm focused on taking the place in. I want to remember as many details as I can, so that I can show Harmony that I have been here.

As we walk down into the main barn, I hear tense male voices from inside.

"Those horses belong to me, Christian!"

"Christian?" Kayla yells out.

"Kayla?"

In the barn aisle are two men—one young and good-looking, wearing a polo shirt, breeches, and cap. He's tall with blond wavy hair and warm brown eyes, but his arms are crossed and he looks like he's about ready to punch the other guy, whose big belly reminds me of my junior-high math teacher. Everyone said Mr. Rhoades enjoyed his beers and burgers. I think this guy might, too.

The man who has to be Christian says, "No, Jim, they are definitely not your horses."

I take note of a cute palomino quarter horse sticking his nose out one of the stalls.

"The hell they aren't! I was my sister's only sibling, and those animals belong to me. I want all of them back. Or I'll take the money they're sold for. That's rightfully mine."

"Hey, what's going on here?" Kayla asks.

"I am sorry you have to see this spectacle, Kayla." He comes toward me with his hand outstretched. "I am Christian Albright."

I smile. "Nice to meet you. I'm Vivienne Taylor."

The other man continues to fume. "This is lovely, folks. It really is. But I want my goddamn horses!"

Christian turns on his heels and is suddenly right in this Jim guy's face. Kayla and I both step back. "Those horses belonged to your sister. You never did a damn thing for Serena. She told me that you never even called her in the last five years. The horses belong to me."

"Was there a will? I was told there was no will!"

"Who told you that?" Christian asks.

"Well . . ."

Christian holds up a hand. "That's what I thought. You're just running your mouth and making assumptions. Your sister *did* have a will. When we got engaged, she had a will drawn up and made me the beneficiary. She gave me the authority to keep, sell, or donate horses as I saw fit."

"This is wrong! I'm family. You're . . . you're just—" Jim is turning bright red, and the bulge in his stomach is jiggling.

I glance at Kayla, who looks as stricken as I feel.

"I'm going to fight this. You'll be hearing from my attorney."

"Fine by me," Christian shoots back. "Go right ahead and waste your time and money. Won't change a thing."

Jim storms off, and a moment later we hear the turn of an engine.

"I am sorry, ladies. This has been an ugly mess. On top of losing Serena, I've had to deal with *relatives* like him coming out of the woodwork."

"I'm sorry," Kayla says. She rubs his shoulder.

"Luckily Serena was smart enough to draw that will up. She actually did that only a few months ago, at my urging. I had my will updated when we got engaged. I was surprised when she told me that she didn't have one. She thought that because she didn't have a family yet, she didn't really need one. But I told her that she had a family. The horses. And me." He is tearing up. "I miss her so much. Our entire future together was gone in that moment. I am so angry that I missed my flight that day. I told her to leave what needed fixing around here until I could get here. But she was so damn independent."

"Yes, she was," Kayla replies.

I have no idea what they're talking about, but I'm really curious now about how Dr. Miller died. When Kayla had mentioned *accident*, I assumed *car accident*.

Kayla lays a hand on my shoulder. "You'll be happy to know that Vivienne is riding Harmony. Vivienne is our scholarship recipient this year, and an absolutely fabulous rider."

"That's good to hear. Congratulations." He wipes the tears from his face. "Harmony is a fine horse. A bit high-strung, but if Kayla handed the reins to you, she has faith you can handle her."

"She's a wonderful horse. Very athletic." God, I want so badly to ask him what her full history is, but I feel too awkward to ask right now.

"I suppose you ladies are here to collect the blankets," he says. "It'll start cooling down in the next few weeks. Hopefully I will be back East by then to close escrow on our . . . my place."

"Serena told me all about the property you guys were buying and what you wanted to do with it." Kayla smiles in what looks to be an attempt to comfort him.

"Yeah. Well." He rubs his hands together. "Let me get your things. And Timmy? How is our big guy doing?"

"Fabulous. I love him. Thank you."

"I know Serena would be happy that you have him."

I feel so bad for this guy. I can't even imagine what it would be like to lose the person you'd planned to spend your entire life with, all the plans they must have made.

We follow Christian into the tack room, where a few boxes are stacked and sealed up.

"You packing this place up on your own?" Kayla asks.

"Yeah."

"Do you want some help?"

"No. Thank you. In a strange way, going through all of this is kind of healing. I feel like she's here with me."

Kayla nods.

"That box there has both Harmony and Timmy's blankets. I can carry it out for you."

"Sure. Thank you."

We walk back to the Range Rover, and Christian sets the box in back. Then he turns to me. "You know what? I almost forgot, there's a really nice leather halter with Harmony's name on it in the tack room. I think it's hanging on the left-hand side. Would you want to have it?"

"Of course," I reply. "Thanks."

I run back down to the tack room and decide to say hello to Bart, the little palomino. Harmony's nameplate is still on the stall door directly across from his. "Hey Bart, how are you?" I rub my hands down his face. His ears prick forward. "I have your friend Harmony now." I bring an image of Harmony up in my mind. "She is afraid of something. Do you know what she's afraid of?"

*The man.*

Oh boy! That was clear! "Which man?"

*He is a bad man. Do you have a carrot?*

"Is that all you have for me?"

*I still want a carrot.*

I look around to see if there are any horse treats and find a bag of pellets. I feed a couple to him. "Sorry. Can't find any carrots."

*These are good. The man is bad. Good night.*

Bart may not be the smartest horse. He isn't like Harmony, who I sense is very intelligent but too afraid to communicate. I thank him again and collect the halter, which is really nice.

The barn light shines out onto Christian and Kayla. *Whoa!* They're in an embrace. And it is not just your average friendly goodbye hug. No way.

I step back but take a longer look.

Yep.

I get the feeling that Kayla and Christian are more than just friends.

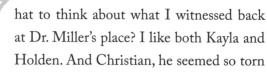

## CHAPTER twenty-one

What to think about what I witnessed back at Dr. Miller's place? I like both Kayla and Holden. And Christian, he seemed so torn up about Dr. Miller's death. None of it makes any sense. And what about what Bart "told" me about Harmony and the bad man?

Who was this bad man? Harmony had shown me a baseball cap. Christian had a baseball cap on today, and he once had Harmony in his barn. Had he been abusive to my mare? And there was the ladder that Timmy had shown me, the one I had been dreaming about.

"I'm sorry you had to see all of that," Kayla says, breaking into my thoughts. "There are greedy people who come out of the woodwork when people die and who think they are owed something just because they're related. Serena's brother Jim is a loser who has done nothing with his life. It is good that Christian had Serena draw up that will.

"Anyway, it's all adult drama. Nothing for you to be concerned with." She pulls into an In-N-Out Burger. "You have to have one of these burgers. They're a California institution."

"Sounds good to me." I try to take the nervous edge out of my voice.

We eat our burgers and fries, and as I am wiping my hands off, she says, "I have a proposition for you."

"Okay."

"We do some work with Christian, and as you know, he is renowned and a fine coach. Holden and I have asked him if he would be willing either to come out to Fairmont next summer and coach the Young Equestrians team, or, if he can't make it out here, to have that same group come out and work with him in Virginia. The way time flies, next summer will be here before you know it. One way or the other we do plan to put this program into effect, and because you received the scholarship, we want to extend Christian's program to you next summer."

I am speechless. "Really?" I finally squeak.

"Really. You are one of the most talented young riders I have seen in a long time, Vivienne. And your essay about what you want to do in the future was so impressive, you are definitely at the top of the list. We'll only be able to send six of you, but just know that you will likely be one of the six. That is, if you want to do it."

"Oh my gosh! Yes. That would be incredible." I can't believe what she's offering me. But wait, I had planned to be home over the summer. Dean. Mom. Cole. The crew. "But . . ."

"Is something wrong?" she asks.

"I don't know if my family can afford it."

"As I said, it would be included in the scholarship. But you have to maintain your grades, and obviously how well you do this year as a competitor will play into it."

Wow. That she and Holden would offer this to me is mind-blowing. Then I think about Holden and what I just saw. And I pray that it isn't what it looked like between Kayla and Christian.

"This is really incredible. Thank you." I take a sip from my soda and decide that since Kayla and I are here alone and chatting, I'll just go ahead and ask what I've been wanting to know all evening. "I hate to ask this—or even change subjects, because this is really exciting—but can I ask you something?"

"Shoot."

"What exactly happened to Dr. Miller? How did she die?"

Kayla sets her napkin down. "Serena was apparently up on the ladder changing lightbulbs in the barn. She lost her balance. The ladder came down, and so did she. She hit her head hard and that was it. No one really knows if she lost her balance and then the ladder fell with her, or if the ladder was just not stable. I guess no one will ever know."

I stare at her. My hands are cold and my stomach suddenly hurts.

"Vivienne? You okay? You look a little pale."

"I'm sorry. That is just so awful. Do you think any of the horses saw what happened?"

"Probably. But it's not like they can fill us in on any of it." She raises an eyebrow, and in that split second I wonder if she knows what I know: that horses *can* talk.

"Right." It makes some sense to me now. Harmony witnessed

Serena falling off the ladder and dying. It has traumatized her badly. The situation around the "bad man" is still confusing. It could easily be a separate piece of information that Bart, the palomino quarter horse, gave me. It could be as simple as Harmony not liking men who wear baseball caps. Maybe a ranch hand at one time had worn one, and she'd been in his way while cleaning corrals, and he'd poked her with a rake.

But I also have another thought. It's quite a bit more sinister. I can't help wondering if the ladder, the man in the cap, and Dr. Serena Miller's death are somehow entwined.

CHAPTER *twenty-two*

Friday arrives, and I am thrilled to be having my first lesson out on cross-country with Newman Becker. Actually, I'm beginning to get a handle on each riding instructor's style. Holden is tough and analytic. He likes to pose a lot of questions to his students and expects them to know the answers on cue. When a student answers correctly or is riding well, he is full of praise.

Kayla is always enthusiastic and tends to work from a positive reinforcement angle. If you aren't getting a lot of praise from her, you know there's something you need to work on. She allows her students time to figure out what needs to be corrected before gently nudging them in the right direction. After every lesson, she goes over what each of us should be focusing on. There are times when she'll ask one or the other of us *individually* to give instructions. I have not been asked to be the instructor of the day yet, and I have not been a victim of an instructor of the day. Kayla also has us take turns videotaping one another so we can view the videos later.

Then there is my idol—Newman Becker. As mentioned, he can be a bit hard to take. Newman has a completely different style from either Holden or Kayla. It's one that I'm going to have to get used to. He doesn't usually praise, and he yells a lot. But the yelling seems to be effective, as it appears to scare the crap out of most of us. And I think everyone wants to impress Newman. He seems impressed by Lydia. I receive an occasional "good job," but I know I'm not his favorite. Newman tends to favor the kids who belong in the DZ, and I am curious why. Has being an Olympian made him a snob?

Nonetheless, I want badly to impress Newman. In my five stadium lessons with him so far, Harmony and I have done a decent job, but cross-country always steps things up a notch. Our first event is only a week away. Per the curriculum, we will have an event at the school once a month. The first event will be a two-day: dressage and stadium on Friday, cross-country on Saturday. Sunday is the Homecoming dance, and we'll have Monday off. Because of our sport, Fairmont doesn't follow the traditional school calendar.

These two- and three-day events will factor into the selection of Fairmont's Young Equestrian team in my senior year. The team travels and competes outside of the academy and at major events. Only seniors are on the team. Thus, I'm nervous.

I'm happy that Riley is in my group for the day out on cross-country. I am not happy that Tristan and Lydia are, too.

As I tack up Harmony, I whisper to her, "I met Bart." I show her his face.

*Darkness.* Oh God, are we back to square one? Then I get—

*He's not the sharpest tool in the barn.* I laugh, hoping she will feed off my happy energy.

I place the saddle on her back. "He told me about a bad man, Harmony. That you're afraid of a bad man."

Her body tenses. Veins pop out on her neck, and she moves uneasily in the cross-ties. "Hey, it's okay." I stroke her neck. "Can you tell me who the man is?"

Now, the black darkness turns to red, as if a bucket of red paint has been tossed onto it. The thing is, I am pretty sure that it's blood. I so want to continue asking her, but her anxiety is rising, and the last thing I need out on cross-country is a wound-up horse.

"Hey, Vivvie, you ready?" Riley rides up on his horse, Santos.

"Yeah. Let me just get her bridle on."

We have been told to spend fifteen minutes in the warm-up arena before meeting Newman down at the start box.

Tristan and Lydia are already there, and she's laughing at something he's saying. He looks at us and smiles.

I put Harmony to work. After fifteen minutes, we make our way out to the course. Lydia rides up next to me. "Isn't this sweet? Me and Tristan? You and Riley?" She giggles.

I glance past her without responding.

"Oh, what, you're too good for me to make small talk? I'm only being friendly."

I eye her as Harmony sets the pace. "You haven't been friendly toward me since the day I got here. I'm hugely doubtful that you want to start now."

"Fine. Have it your way. I just thought that since our guys are roommates and all that, maybe you and I could try and be friends. I could give you a makeover, and then you could come sit with us at lunch and dinner. We all miss Riley."

"Lydia, I don't want a makeover. I don't want to eat lunch or dinner with you. And Riley and I are just friends."

"Really? Just friends, huh? Oh, I get it. You are *those* kinds of friends."

"What?"

"Word travels fast around here." She puts her mare into a trot and moves ahead of me.

I don't want to think what I'm thinking, but I've been in high school, and even though the crowd I used to run with is very different from any of the kids at Fairmont, I do know that rumors happen. Is there a rumor going around that Riley and I are sleeping together? I glance over at Riley, who has already made it down to Newman. Boy, he and I have a lot to discuss. Tristan made a similar comment to me as well. Why is everyone under the impression that Riley and I are a *thing*?

Newman stuffs his hands into the pockets of his breeches and looks over at all of us. "Okay. Tristan, you're up. Let's do the log first, to the roll top, and then into the water and out over the brush."

Tristan and Sebastian are in the start box. Newman gives them the ten-second countdown. Their ride is essentially perfect. Lydia claps her hands.

And me? All I can think is, *Oh my God! They are so beautiful!* Then I remind myself how much I do not like Tristan.

"Nice," is all Newman says.

As Lydia heads to the start box, Tristan winks at me! He actually freaking *winks,* oh-so-casually, at me! What the hell? I look down at Harmony's mane.

Lydia has a beautiful ride, too. Ah, well.

Riley goes next. Santos refuses at the roll top. Newman yells, "Where were your eyes? How long have you been riding, Riley, and you look down? What the hell is wrong with you? What do you think that beast is going to do when you look down? Are you an idiot? You look like an idiot! Come back around and do it the right way!"

See what I mean? I feel really bad for Riley. But he circles around, clears the jump, and takes the other two smoothly. Even as he trots back, Newman continues to berate. "You want to become a top rider, Reed? Not like that, you won't! Maybe I should send you back to beginner novice! You got work to do if you don't want to waste your parents' money, son. All right, Vivienne, you're up."

God. My poor friend. Riley's face is red, and he looks a bit like a beaten dog. I know that Newman's words must have hurt his pride, and I want to comfort him. But, I need to focus now. As I set out toward the log, I feel hesitation from Harmony, so I put my leg on and give her some encouragement. She takes off a stride early at the jump, but clears it. I do a better job setting her up and riding her to the roll top. Coming out of the water and over the brush, she finally is in a groove, and we feel in sync as she flies over it. I know I'm going to get blasted for the log, but I am still elated, because as we come off the brush it's clear to me that this mare can easily take me up through prelim and beyond. Her scope is awesome. I pat her on her the neck. "Good girl. Good girl."

I ride up to Newman, who between pursed lips gives me, "Horrid ride over the log. You need to ride her to it. What was the hesitation all about?" He crosses his arms. "I'll tell you what it was about—confidence. You have to ride this horse with confidence.

I'm not seeing that out there. If you want to keep your scholarship, you better learn to ride to the fence and set that horse up properly. Okay, let's move on."

I just nod. Newman is right about the first fence, but the rest of it was damn good, and I am thrilled to learn that Harmony is as athletic as I had hoped she'd be.

The rest of the lesson goes pretty well for me, but Riley continues to have a rough time of it. By the time we're told to walk back and cool the horses off, I want to hug him—and ask him if he started a rumor about the two of us. Kind of conflicting impulses.

"You okay?" I finally ask.

"That guy is such a hardass."

"That, he is."

"You know what, let's ride over to the Olympic House. I don't want to go back yet," Riley says.

"Okay, I've been wanting to get out there."

"As Horace said, let's 'seize the day,'" he replies.

"Actually, Horace would say 'carpe diem.'"

"Damn, you know your Latin, too?"

"I *am* here on scholarship."

"She rides! She thinks!"

We both laugh, and Newman's negativity is left behind. "I just have to be back in an hour. I'm going with Martina to her parents' house tonight for dinner."

"Nice!" he says, then sighs. "Mine will be here tomorrow for parents' day."

"You don't sound too happy."

He shrugs slightly. "My dad is . . . difficult."

"Yeah. I get that."

We leave it at that and continue to ride. I begin to relax. The air is warm, the soil a reddish clay color against the backdrop of greenery, and I can see the ocean out in the distance. I remind myself what a lucky girl I am.

Since it's only Riley and me and he seems to have mellowed out from his scolding, I finally say, "Hey, Ri?"

"Yeah?"

"Lydia made some kind of remark about us being together, implying that we're having sex—and that other kids are talking about it."

"Oh man! Don't listen to her. She will do whatever she can to get under your skin, Vivvie. She's probably the one who started the rumor—if there really is one. I'll do what I can to set it straight."

"Thanks. I'm actually . . . I'm a virgin."

"Makes two of us."

"Really?"

"Really," he replies. "Hey, maybe we should let them all think we're doing it."

"Riley!"

"Giving you a hard time, Viv. Relax. Here we are."

We come upon a stone cabin. There's a porch out front, and around back, a two-stall barn. "Looks kind of haunted," I say.

"Perhaps it is." He wiggles his eyebrows.

I slide off Harmony. We put the horses in the open stalls.

"Come on," he says.

The place is unlocked and kind of dusty. There is a table and four chairs, a small kitchen, and an old sofa in front of a fireplace. As I look around, I'm mesmerized. There are photos of Olympians and their horses going all the way back to the 1930s.

I stop in front of Newman's photo. "This is cool."

"He's still a hardass."

"I agree, but—Riley!"

"What?"

"We should film some of our documentary here for our history project. Think of it. Inside the Olympic House. We can interview Newman."

"You can do that part."

"Fine. But we can totally ace this thing."

"Maybe," he says. He walks over to the fridge and takes out some sodas, handing me one.

"Thanks."

"I think it's a good idea," he continues. "You know we'll have to be careful. Word on campus is that Lydia is twisting Tristan's arm to bring her here for their first time. We wouldn't want to stumble on that scene."

"No, we wouldn't." This info gives me an odd feeling that I can't quite name. "You think that's true?"

"Don't know. Don't care. I just like coming here to think. No one comes out here."

"Looks like someone does." I spot a jacket on one of the chairs.

"I think that's Holden's. I haven't seen it on him for a while. The chill doesn't set in around here until November. I bet he hasn't even missed it."

I pick it up. It's dark green and has the Fairmont logo on the back. "Huh. It looks like there's some blood on it. Some kind of stain, anyway."

"Maybe we should take it to him," Riley says. "See if it's his."

"Okay. We better get back. I don't want to be late for Martina."

"Yep."

I'm finding it kind of odd that Riley has brought me out to the Olympic House. I feel like I did the other day when he asked me to the Homecoming dance—as if he had something he wanted to say to me. But it's not like I am with horses; I could be wrong about what I'm sensing.

Back at the stalls, I set the jacket down on top of the stall door. As Harmony turns to face me, she sees it and begins weaving and snorting. "Hey, hey."

"What's wrong with her?" Riley asks.

"Here, take this. Can you put it out of sight?" I hand him the jacket. "She's being weird."

I turn back to Harmony. "What is it? What is it, my girl?"

Black to red to the cap. And then to the jacket. She shows me the jacket. Then the blood on it. She shows me the blood on it. Then darkness once again.

I have an awful thought.

What if Holden Fairmont is the bad man? Why *is* there blood on Holden's jacket—if it is his—and why did Harmony specifically just show me the blood?

I calm her down before I get back on her, but I'm scared. Scared now that something really terrible happened the night that Dr. Miller died. Is Holden Fairmont involved in his cousin's death?

CHAPTER *twenty-three*

ristan had been impressed by both Vivvie and her horse out on cross-country today—well, especially Vivvie. Lydia can ride. There's no denying it. But Vivienne has a certain finesse; as if she and Harmony just meld together as one. Definitely impressive and . . . beautiful.

He closes Sebastian's stall door, noting that Vivienne and Riley aren't back yet. He had seen them ride out in the opposite direction.

*Wonder what those two are up to?*

When he turns around from locking the stall, there stands Lydia, hands on hips. "Hey! You sneaking up on me?" he says.

"You like her!" she spits.

"Who?"

"You know who! You like *Scholarship*."

*Oh, crap.* "I don't," he lies.

"Right. Don't think I haven't noticed the way you look at her when she rides. Like you're all amazed!"

"She's just, just a really good rider."

"Please!"

"Lydia, calm down. You know you're my girlfriend."

"Yeah. I am. But have you even made any plans for *us*? For Homecoming? I would think you'd want to go all out. Me and you are the perfect couple. Vivienne Taylor—she's a total Wal-Martian. And *I* am the one who knows about your family, the one you trusted to tell all that *stuff* to."

Tristan takes a step back and assesses the steely, hard look in Lydia's eyes. "What does *that* mean?"

She shrugs. "That I am only looking out for you, Tristan. That's how you *should* take it. I want what is best for you, and *I* am best for you." She stands on her tiptoes and kisses him. Her lips feel poisonous. He stiffens, and she pulls away. "Play nice with me. Don't screw this up." Then she spins and flounces out of the barn.

*God, I am so . . . trapped.*

He stands stunned, lowering his head as a mixture of emotions shoots through him.

When he looks up, Vivienne is walking in with Harmony.

"You guys go on a trail ride?" he asks.

"Uh-huh."

"It's nice out there, huh?"

"It is." She takes the saddle off Harmony.

He walks up to her and places his hands over hers on the saddle. "Here, let me put this up for you."

She looks up at him. The blue in her eyes is *so* blue, like cornflower, and for a second he feels something wonderful and intense between them. She's not moving her hands from underneath his. Not yet. Finally she says, "I've got this."

"Oh, come on, Vivienne."

"All right. Thanks." She lets him take her saddle.

When he comes back, she's brushing Harmony down. "She sure is beautiful," he says, his voice catching a bit on that last word.

"She is."

"And talented."

"Yep. That, too."

"So are you, Vivienne."

Vivienne stops brushing and stands up straight, but she doesn't look him in the eye as he stares at her with a hungry look. "Tristan, please—what do you want from me?" she whispers. "You have a *girlfriend*, and I . . . I *can't* get mixed up in a hot mess between you two."

He looks away. *Damn. She's right.* There's Riley, whom he didn't want to hurt. And Lydia—she would lash out like a crazed tiger. She could—and would?—ruin him. But . . . he likes this girl. A lot. "If there was no Lydia and me, would it be possible? You and me?"

She goes back to brushing Harmony. Several silent seconds stretch between them. Finally she says, sounding slightly sad, "I'm sorry, Tristan, but even then it wouldn't be possible."

He wants to say that he doesn't believe her. He wants to tell her that he will change her mind, that she is all he thinks about and it is practically killing him. So . . .

"Hey, you guys. How much did I suck out there today?" says Riley, leading Santos toward his stall.

Tristan claps Riley on the shoulder. "Dude, you just had an off day. Newman knows, we all know, that you're talented."

"Thanks, bro."

"Bye, Vivienne. Nice riding with you guys today," he says before walking out of the barn.

"Oh . . . I mean . . . thank you," she replies.

On the way back to the dorm, Tristan imagines the what-ifs: What if Riley hadn't walked in? What if he told Vivienne that he didn't believe that she never thought about him *that way*? What if he had just gone for it and kissed her instead of asking her that question? But he knows all this is pure fantasy. Maybe Vivienne has just told him the truth. And, maybe getting out of his mess with Lydia is damn near impossible.

*Question is: How much of a risk am I willing to take?*

# RILEY

CHAPTER *twenty-four*

Although it's a Friday night, Riley tries hard to focus on his homework—and not on his parent arrival tomorrow morning. They come every damn year for Parents' Day weekend. Every year it is the same browbeating, the same five hundred thousand questions, the boring-ass lecture about how much they pay for him to attend Fairmont—blah, blah, and blah.

*Big question to self: Why stick with Fairmont?*

But then he reminds himself what living in his parents' home and going to school in Virginia was like. Becker-the-pecker can call him an idiot a thousand times; Fairmont will still be worth it.

As Riley gazes out at his dorm room window's ocean view, his phone chirps, indicating an incoming text.

*You in?* It's from Nate Deacon. Riley's stomach sinks.

Riley likes to bet. He is a good gambler. Last year, from the standing poker game he and some other guys on campus kept hidden from the administration, he amassed something like fourteen grand. This money, it is going to buy his freedom. He *needs* to keep his winning streak going. If he can maintain it, he will graduate with enough to move far away and start a new life, finally out from under his dad's heavy thumb.

But this bet . . . Vivienne truly is his friend, and he knows she will be hurt, and mortified.

He also knows that Vivvie has a thing for Tristan, and vice versa. He hasn't said anything to her about it yet, but when those two are in close proximity, the heat is way too obvious. Riley admires Tristan for not trying to cross that line. Of course, Lydia will skin him alive if he does, him and Vivienne both.

Riley's phone chirps again.

*Damn Nate!* Riley flips open his phone. "Dude, I *don't* think it's cool. I *don't* want to do it!"

"Riley?"

"Oh, Dad. Hi. Sorry, sir. I thought you were someone else."

Now Riley leans back in his chair and watches the moonlit tide go in and out, in and out.

"Your mother and I will be there at ten a.m. sharp. Be on time and dressed appropriately."

"Yes, sir."

"I'll have a guest with us."

Riley sits up. "Who?"

"Joel Parker. He wanted to join us and see how you're doing. He's considering colleges in that area. We invited him along. He may even transfer to Fairmont for his senior year."

"Okay."

"*Okay?* Joel has been your friend since you guys were like what,

six? And 'okay' is all you can say? We thought you would be delight-
ed by this."

"Sorry, sir. It's just, I've been studying and you caught me off
guard."

"Well, you better be on your guard tomorrow. Ten a.m.—sharp."

Riley hangs up his phone, closes his eyes. A minute later another
text comes in. *FIFTEEN grand now, bro! You in?*

Riley takes a deep breath, feeling slightly dizzy and a little sick.
He pecks out *Yeah. I'm in.*

CHAPTER *twenty-five*

'm trying so hard to focus on Martina's conversation as she drives us to her parents' place in Bel Air. But inside, my mind is such a whirl.

*If there was no Lydia and me . . . You and me?*

But I meant what I'd said to him. Didn't I?

Oh, God! Tristan Goode will screw up all my hopes, goals, and dreams. I just know he will.

Then there's this thing with Harmony—the blood on the jacket, the cap, Christian and Kayla, Dr. Miller's death, my poor, traumatized horse.

"You okay?" Martina asks.

"Oh, of course."

"Well, I was just blabbing to you about the event coming up, asking you how cross-country was today, and you just kept looking out the window."

"I'm sorry, M. I am a little . . . preoccupied."

"Look, I know we've only known each other a few weeks, Vivvie, but you're kind of easy to read. What's going on?"

I take a deep breath. "If I tell you, you have to promise not to say anything."

"Promise."

"I think that maybe something really bad happened to Dr. Miller."

"Well, of course it did. She died."

"But I don't think it was an accident."

"What do you mean?"

I start to babble. "See, Harmony is still nervous with me, and when she sees a baseball cap she freaks out, and today Riley and I went over to the Olympic House and there was a jacket with blood on it that Riley thinks might belong to Holden and—"

"Wait. *So* . . . because a horse freaks out over a baseball cap and because Holden's jacket has blood on it, you think that he murdered his cousin?"

When she puts it like that, I know it sounds ridiculous. But I can't tell her about Bart telling me about the bad man and the images Harmony and Timmy shared with me. "I didn't say murder, exactly."

"Murder was implied."

I laugh. "Silly, huh?"

Martina gives me a "I forgive you for being crazy" smile. So nice. "I know that Dr. Miller and Holden didn't always get along. Holden is more into natural healing than she was. I heard them argue once about it, but I still think she just had a terrible, freaky accident. As far as Harmony goes, horses can be emotional. You know that. I always think about how these big, strong animals can be startled by a blowing leaf."

I nod. "That's so true."

As our conversation drifts back into tamer territory, I consider Martina's perspective. I still don't think I'm altogether *wrong* exactly, but could Harmony have misunderstood the incident as something sinister when maybe it was just a horrible, upsetting accident?

"Here we are!" Martina presses a clicker, and an ornate wrought-iron gate opens up.

We drive up a circular drive and—it's just incredible. Perfectly manicured landscaping, a water fountain with a giant stone fish in the center, and a massive Spanish-style home, all lit up like a Christmas tree.

"Come meet my mom and dad."

I am frozen with sensory overload, but Martina grabs my hand, leads me up the steps, and opens a set of massive, carved wooden doors. We step into a foyer tiled with cream-colored marble. There are *two* staircases and a humongous chandelier, and it all looks like something out of a movie.

"Martina? Is that you, sweetheart?" A woman with a slight Spanish accent calls out.

"Down here, Mommy."

My stomach is filled with all sorts of nerves. I am about to meet Erika Martín! The totally famous, great actress!

Must. Remember. To Breathe.

She stands at the top of the stairs, her long, wavy black hair trailing down past her shoulders. She's wearing a white flowy blouse, a pair of jeans, and the perfect amount of sparkly jewelry. She's perfect.

She kisses Martina on both cheeks. "Ah, Mija! We've missed you so much. Your father is out back at the barbecue, making your favorite."

"Ribs!" Martina claps and rubs her hands together. "This is Vivienne, my friend and new roommate."

Erika Martín wraps her arms around me and hugs me tight. "Welcome, Vivienne! I am so happy you could join us for dinner. Come on, girls. Come out and see your daddy."

Am I dreaming? I have to be. I pinch myself—twice. Nope. Not dreaming. This is real.

I follow them through the family room—it's big but still looks nice and comfy. The walls are done up in warm golds and peaches. There are overstuffed suede and leather sofas and chairs, and it all opens up to a large family-style kitchen. It's got everything, but it isn't really like a magazine picture—this kitchen looks like it actually gets used. At the counter is a set of leather bar stools and behind that I count one, two . . . three ovens.

We walk past the kitchen through arched glass doors to a tiled patio lit with jillions of candles. The sun is setting in the west, casting a glow over the area. I inhale the scent of the rose garden next to the outdoor kitchen. And of course there's a pool, shiny and serene in the evening light, flowing down into what looks like—a canyon?

"Mija!" Martina's father, dressed in a chef's cap and apron, comes out from behind the grill. He and Martina have the same bright smile. He just lights up upon seeing her.

*So nice. Must be so nice.*

"Papi!" Martina runs and throws her arms around him.

"My Martina-beena! And who is your friend?" he asks.

"This is Vivienne," Martina says, "my new roommate."

"Nice to meet you. I am Rodrigo Lunes." He wipes his free hand on his apron. "Sorry, my hands are a bit smoky."

This family, they are so real and wonderful. The delectable smell of barbecue wafts our way, and my stomach goes *grrrgle*.

"How about you girls mix up the fruit salad?" he asks. "Mommy is going to finish her famous flan for dessert."

"I've missed you guys," Martina says. "Vivienne, you up for making the salad?"

"Just hand me a knife and bowl."

During dinner, Martina's mother tells us all about her recent movie that's filming in Sweden. Her dad tells how on his trip to Africa last month, where he produced a documentary for IMAX theaters on the wildebeest migration, he woke up to find a baboon in his hotel room. They are *so* interesting . . . and even interested in me, my life, too. Completely different from the way all those shiny magazines make them out to be.

"So, do you like Fairmont?" Martina's mom asks me.

"I do. It's an adjustment. My small town in Oregon, well, it's a *small* town."

"I get that. I am from teeny-tiny Colima, Mexico. Can you imagine when I came here what it was like for me? I think I do understand, Mija."

I smile. It's like having a little bit of my own mom back.

"Vivvie has already had the honor of being harassed by Lydia Gallagher and her coven," Martina said.

Her mom waves a hand as if batting away flies. "Don't pay any mind to those girls. They are just jealous, I am sure."

"I don't know about that. Some of them are really good riders."

"They were so rotten to my Martina her freshman year."

"*Ma-mi!*" Martina shakes her head.

"I'm sorry, Mija. I know I told you I wouldn't talk about it." She smiles and looks at me. "I am happy that Martina has made such a nice new friend, Vivienne. You girls can look out for each other."

I am dying to know what Lydia and the DZ did to Martina. But if Martina wants to tell me, then she will. However, let any one of those stupid girls try to pull any new crap on my friend and they'll find out what kind of a smackdown a small-town girl from Oregon can pack.

"I am going to get dessert." Martina's father stands up and heads into the house. A moment later, we hear him yelling, "Erika! Erika! Come here quick!"

Martina's mom jumps up and runs into the house, and after a moment's hesitation, Martina and I run after her.

Erika and Rodrigo are standing in front of a computer at a built-in desk in the kitchen.

"That son of a bitch. I am going to find him, Erika!"

Martina's mother is rubbing his shoulder. "Rodrigo, no. Let the police handle it."

"This has been going on for six months!"

"Mom, this does seem excessive," Martina says.

"Honey, it's just some crazy idiot. You know how it is," she says. "Nothing for you to worry about. Go, be with your friend."

Martina walks back to the patio and motions for me to sit by her. "I'm sorry about that," she says.

"Is everything . . . what's going on?" I ask.

"Oh, some idiot has been sending e-mails for months to my mother, stalking her. Then, about a month ago, she received a box of dead roses. Whoever it is writes that he is watching her. That sort of thing."

"It sounds scary."

Martina's shoulders tense. "It's show business. My parents have the police working on it, and they have put extra security around here and around her."

"But still . . ."

She nods. "It does scare me. But the thing is, I just don't want to talk about this. I'm just glad, like my mom is, that you're my friend."

"Sure. No worries. I'm happy we're friends, too."

"Want to go for a swim?"

"Sounds perfect."

We head inside to change into our suits. As I float in the warm pool with the stars sparkling overhead, I think about how everybody seems to have secrets they'd do anything to keep hidden—and that nothing and no one is exactly how they seem to be on the outside.

CHAPTER *twenty-six*

Parents' Day!

Minus the exclamation point for me.

Parents' Day.

I admit it—I'm feeling down that my mom can't attend. I get why, of course. Mom would be at Fairmont today if is there was any way she could afford it. Of course, Lane is permanently MIA.

Martina's mom and dad are coming down, but instead of being a part of the school program, they'll take Martina to lunch. They invited me to join them, but I don't want to intrude on their family time, especially after last night. That sicko stalker has definitely shaken them up.

All I plan to do today is study and make a visit to Harmony.

Just as I am sitting down at my desk, books open, I receive this text from Riley: *PLEASE come meet my parents.*

*I'm studying,* I write back.

*PLEASE! J 911! Save me! Meet us at the fountain.*

Okay. That sounds kind of ominous. Riley has vaguely mentioned that he has some issues with his dad. When he said it in passing, I said, "Everyone has issues with their dad."

A desperate friend, father issues. The whole pleading thing. I text back: *OKAY. You owe me!*

I'm not always a great meet-the-parents kind of kid. Martina's parents were so warm and welcoming that my nerves dissipated quickly. Typically though, I am on the shy side, and today I am bloated, feel gross because my boobs hurt, and I have a massive zit building on my chin. Oh thanks be to the Goddess Premenstrual. That bitch.

After I rescue Riley, I am so going to find myself a chocolate bar.

On my way down to the fountain, I run into Lydia Gallagher, arm-in-arm with some guy. Blond, blue-eyed, an all-American type—maybe a relative?

"Oh, hi there, Vivienne Taylor," she says as I scurry past.

"Yes?" I stop and turn around.

"This is my brother, Daniel."

"Nice to meet you."

"Good morning, Ms. Taylor," he says, stretching out his hand to me, but in this very to-the-manor born way.

"Daniel, Vivienne received the scholarship this year. Her roommate is Tina." She tilts her head and gives a little knowing smirk.

"Very nice to meet you. Please tell Tina that I say hello."

"You mean Martina?" I ask.

"She always let me call her Tina," he replies.

At this comment, he and Lydia both start giggling.

"Okay. I have to go. Nice to meet you." *Lie.*

"Oh, it was my pleasure," he says, and they stroll away, cackling over some inside joke clued-in people like them always seem to have. *Why do I always have to feel so . . . off balance around that girl?* I also feel a rush of affection for my little brother, Cole, who though consistently annoying is really a sweet kid.

Over by one of the big fountains I see Riley with an older couple. His grandparents? But wait, Riley mentioned that he's the youngest of five kids. There's another guy with them, around our age. One of his brothers?

His dad looks kind of *formal*—tall, thin, one of those skinny mustaches, a serious-looking suit and tie. His mom, shorter and a little more relaxed looking, is also wearing a suit—and so is Riley. The possible brother-guy has more of a prepster style—short hair, khakis, a pink polo shirt, and an argyle vest. Someone is shooting for the Ivy League.

I have on jeans. With one of my nicer blouses, but still.

Then I take a good look around. Most the other families are dressed pretty casually, and I start to understand why Riley needs to be saved.

*Okay, I can do this.*

I walk over to where they are gathered.

"Vivienne!" Riley jumps up and throws his arms around me.

"Whoa! I mean, hi, Ri."

Riley's mother reaches out her hand to me first and in a deeply southern accent says, "Oh, honey, how nice to finally meet you. We've heard so much about you." She pumps my hand and then throws her arms around me too and laughs.

*Phew! Much nicer than I thought.*

"Oh? I hope they were good things," I reply, oh-so-awkwardly.

"Nice to meet you." I smile and try to get Riley to look at me, but he won't.

"Well, aren't you just as darling as Riley said. Vivienne, this is my husband, Mr. Harrison Reed."

Riley's dad turns to me and gives me a once-over. Now I wish I were wearing a suit, too. He has piercing blue eyes just like Riley's, but way more serious and intense.

"Pleased to meet you, Miss Taylor. Riley has mentioned you quite a bit, as my wife said. It's wonderful that you received the scholarship."

"Thank you." Awkwarder and awkwarder. I am actually starting to sweat. And why has Riley been talking about me so much to his parents?

Ivy League cuts in now. "I'm Joel Parker, Vivienne. Riley and I have been friends for years. I'm considering transferring to Fairmont for my senior year next year."

"Oh." I glance at Riley. "Nice. So, you ride?"

"I do. I have a *splendid* Thoroughbred named Libby."

"Wow. That sounds great."

"I expect you will be joining us this evening for dinner," Riley's father says.

"Well, I—"

"Of course, she is!" says Riley. " Vivienne's been dying to meet you, and I want you to get to know . . . my girl." He wraps an arm around me, and oh boy, now I am definitely sweating bullets, and the Joel guy is giving me this odd smirk.

*Don't panic. Keep calm. Do I sound like I'm talking to Harmony?*

"It's all set, then," says Mrs. Reed. "Oh, I am so happy we brought a camera. Our friends will want to get a picture of Riley's first real girlfriend."

As my numb brain scrambles to come up with something normal to say, Riley squeezes my hand hard, and then says, "Well, Mom, Dad, Joel, why don't I take you down to the barn? Santos is doing splendidly."

*Splendidly?* Holy crap! What *is* going on? Who says *splendidly?* I'm staring dumbfounded at Riley.

He gives me just a peck on the cheek. "See you at six thirty."

"Can't w-wait," I sputter, clueless as ever.

And now Riley, his parents, and Ivy League are walking away. Finally. At last. But I still feeling like I am being watched—and, turns out, I am. There is Tristan, just a few yards over, eyeing me. He's obviously not giving all his attention to the guy who must be his dad.

He turns away, and I can't help thinking that Tristan looks as unhappy and confused as I feel right about now.

# TRISTAN

CHAPTER *twenty-seven*

L isten to me, son. I know how important it is for you to be here. I know what's at stake. But if anyone finds out about any of this—well, you know—you would have to leave here and go take care of your mother," Chandler Goode II says under his breath.

Tristan's mother, Jacquelyn, insisted that he not be named after his father. Tristan was a family name on her side. When his mom had some real strength behind her, she typically got her way. Now she is a shell of that woman. He doesn't understand why this has happened to her, or even how. She was once so confident, so vibrant, and now—she wouldn't even leave the house.

His father insists that the signs have been there all along, leading up to his mother's self-imposed house arrest. Has Tristan been so absorbed in his own life over the last few years that he didn't notice the signs?

Tristan can't help but notice Vivienne hanging with Riley and his parents. His heart quickens with just a glance her way. Hs she seen him? Does she care? Of course she doesn't!

"Tristan, do you hear me?" his dad says, running a hand through blond hair that holds just a hint of silver. His father is aging, and surely the stress of what he is involved in has to be taking a physical toll on him. But didn't his father bring this on himself? And now because Tristan is his son, and because of what he has seen and overheard, he has been dragged into this mess. When he first learned what his father and his "partners" were doing, he seriously thought about calling the authorities himself. So, why hasn't he?

He has to consider the men his father does business with. He doesn't know exactly who they are, but he does know that they are ruthless.

"Yeah, Dad, I hear you. I'm not saying anything."

"Good."

"Yep."

"And you haven't told *anyone* what you heard and what you saw?"

Tristan shakes his head, but avoids looking his father in the eyes. "No, Dad. No one knows." *Tristan Alexander Goode—lord of the idiots. Son of a crook. And a first-class liar. Nice. Real nice.*

His father pats him on the shoulder. "Good. Okay then, so how are your studies?"

*Studies? Now he wants to discuss my studies?* Tristan wants so badly to punch the man in the face. He notices Riley walking away with his parents and some other guy, leaving Vivienne standing there stranded, a look of sheer confusion on her face.

What he wouldn't give to go and grab her hand and say, "Let's get the hell out of here!"

"That's a beautiful girl," his dad says, tilting his head toward Vivienne.

"She's a nice girl, too. She got the scholarship."

"Ah. A *real* equestrian."

"What does that mean?" Tristan asks.

"Oh, son, I'm complimenting her. Face it, most kids here come here on Daddy's dime. She earned her slot."

"That's true."

"So can you. Don't take it to mean that you aren't an excellent rider. I know what your sport means to you."

And that is just one of the many key differences between Tristan and his father. He views what Tristan and all of the students do at Fairmont as a sport. For some of the kids that is probably true. For Tristan though, eventing is not simply a sport. The most important aspect of all of it is the relationship he's developed with Sebastian. His mother is the one he credits with teaching him to have a true appreciation for *the horse*. As a somewhat ironic result, Tristan loves his horse more than he loves either of his parents. He loves his horse more than anything in the world. He feels alive when he's around animals in a way that he doesn't feel alive around anything or anyone else—not until he lifted Vivienne up that day she'd passed out in Harmony's stall. In that moment when she stumbled into him, he knew he'd felt more alive than he ever had before.

But as far as the horses are concerned, and especially his horse, the connection is an undeniable one, and so completely opposite of the way his father feels about and deals with animals that once served the kings of the world. His father views them as a means to an end—as sport and as money.

"Aren't you still dating Lydia Gallagher?" his dad asks.

"I am."

"She might be trouble. A girl with looks like that. You just better be careful and watch out for that one. I mean it."

Tristan watches Vivienne walking to her dorm, thinking, *You have no idea how much trouble Lydia could be, Dad. And not just for me. For all of us.*

## CHAPTER twenty-eight

L et me just say that Riley's behavior has me deeply confused, and that family of his? I won't even go into my first impressions of Ivy League Joel Parker, who, even though Riley has known him for years, does not seem all that pleased to see his supposedly close childhood pal.

I'm still not over the word *splendidly*.

And how about Tristan? On the other side of that water fountain, with his dad looking all grim and serious? Then there was the run-in with Lydia and Daniel Gallagher and their strange remark regarding Martina. Hmm . . . Parents' Day at Fairmont seems to have a distinct dark side.

Ah, the heck with it! I decide to get my horse out and go on a trail ride, see if I can't clear my mind of all this weirdness.

When I get to her stall, Harmony sticks her head out for me to put her halter on, but there's no "Hey, how are you? I'm happy to see you. Can I have a carrot?" But for now, I'll take her ears forward and a curious stare over nothing at all.

I tack her up and ride out onto the cross-country course. The sky is a cloudless blue, and it's seventy-five degrees out. I have no complaints about California weather.

But there is something in the air. Something harder for me to name, or measure.

Although all I really want to do is enjoy the ride and the weather, there is something that Harmony and I need to tackle. We are finally alone and in a space where no one will interrupt us.

I begin easy with her. "You are such a good girl. I am so lucky to have you as my horse." I picture me hugging Harmony and then show her an image of a heart. I infuse these images in my mind with an emotion of overwhelming love and respect.

A minute later, the energy around us switches to electrical. She again shows me a broken heart.

"I know. I know, Harmony." I reach my hand down and scratch her neck, twirling her short strands of mane in my gloved fingers. "I know you miss Dr. Miller."

*Serena!*

Her body tenses, and she does one of her little jigs. I laugh. "Okay, then. I will call her Serena from now on."

We continue at a nice pace. The rich brown earth, the warm sun, and the smell of orange blossoms floating through the air keeps us both at ease.

"Harmony, I want to help you. I know you want to tell me what happened to Serena. I don't think that she just fell off that ladder. I know there is a man you're afraid of, and I also know that the baseball cap and jacket scare you." As I speak to her, I do my best to create images in my mind that will correlate. She communicates through images and feeling. "Serena" is her first word.

As we pass through a creek bed, a red-tailed hawk soars high above, seeking out its prey. I watched for a moment—grace, speed, precision, and relentless determination.

Harmony is no longer "talking." I keep trying to reassure her. "It will help you if you tell me what happened to Serena. Trust me."

I receive no response. My heart sinks a little.

As we get closer to home, Harmony shows me a pretty bay horse with a stripe down the face.

"Who is the horse, Harmony? Who is it? Who does it belong to?"

She shows me the back of someone—a girl, I think.

"Who is it, Harmony?"

The image comes. And it is clear.

The girl turns around; her face is stained with tears.

Lydia Gallagher.

CHAPTER *twenty-nine*

Riley is hoping that Vivienne isn't pissed off at him. His stomach is all knotted up as he puts on his suit jacket. His parents, with their rules about what one must wear and how one must act. And, he can't believe they've brought Joel. Yeah, tonight is going to be some kind of uncomfortable. Just a few hours. That's it. That is all he has to get through—the next few hours.

Thank God, his parents didn't on Vivvie for wearing jeans and a blouse this morning. He almost texted her and suggested a dress for dinner, but he was afraid she'd tell him to go screw himself. He was also afraid she wouldn't show up. He couldn't exactly blame her. He was pretty sure that he'd confused her earlier during the day. He'd *had* to tell his parents that Vivienne was his girlfriend.

His mom and dad and Joel are at their hotel and plan to be back in about fifteen minutes. They asked if Joel could just stay with Riley, but he lied and said there was no room.

He checks his watch and decides to head to Vivvie's room.

What will he tell her? He feels sick to his stomach—sick enough to puke.

He's sweating all along his backside by the time he makes the short walk to Vivvie's dorm room.

Upon reaching her door, he hesitates, takes a deep breath, closes his eyes for about ten seconds, and finally knocks.

The door swings open seconds later, and he takes a slight step back because he's shocked! Vivienne Taylor has gone all out. She curled her hair, and is wearing a black dress that his mother will definitely think is too tight. She has makeup on, and her heels make her nearly as tall as him. "Wow!"

She grabs his hand and pulls him into her room. "Wow? Wow? What the hell, Riley?"

"I mean, wow, you look great."

"Thanks. I figured if you've assigned me the part of your girlfriend, then I'll play it, because you looked scared to death of your dad."

He looks down at his shoes. "I am."

"But Ri, we agreed we just wanted to be friends, right? When you asked me to the dance that *was* the deal. I still *only* want that."

"Me, too."

"Then why go and tell your parents that I'm your girlfriend? What gives?"

"Oh shit, I think I'm gonna . . ." He runs to her bathroom and slams the door.

A few seconds later, as he's leaning over the toilet, she knocks. "Riley? What is going on? Are you sick?"

He washes up in the sink, staring at his pale face in the mirror.

His hands shake as he opens the door. He can't even look at her without tears welling up in his eyes.

Vivvie took a step back. "Oh my God, Ri. What is it?"

He can't speak. Everything is stuck in his throat. Vivvie looks so anxious, concerned.

"Whatever it is, you can tell me. I'm sorry I was pissed off at you. You have to tell me, what is it?"

Now the tears stream down his face. Vivvie reaches her hand out and wipes them away, then takes both of his hands. "Hey, it's okay. It is. Whatever it is, it's okay."

"No, it isn't, Vivvie," he whispers. "My parents will disown me if they find out."

"Find out what?" she asks.

"I'm gay, Vivvie. I am gay."

CHAPTER *thirty*

I want to hold Riley's hand all evening and infuse some sort of strength, or compassion, or whatever he needs from me in that moment. I cannot even grasp the concept of a parent being unwilling to accept a child for who they are, although I am not naive enough to realize that this is not a reality in life.

It's in a moment over escargot (snails; I had never had them before—surprisingly delish) that it hits me how lucky I am. I mean, let's face it, I am weird. I'm not getting around that one. I talk to horses. I do. And they talk to me. Mom, she not only accepts me for who I am, she believes me, loves me, lets me decide what I want to do with it. I think we both believe that if word got out about my "gift," I would get a lot of criticism. Some people would make fun of me; others might hound me to talk to their horses. I'm not ready for any of that.

What would happen to Riley if he "outed" himself? I am thinking about all of this as the waiter brings our entrees. Earlier, his father raised an eyebrow when Riley took my hand. To me, it looked like a warning.

Joel has been scowling at me pretty much all night, and anytime Riley speaks, the guy is all eyes and ears.

I wonder if he and Riley . . .

Oh. *Oh.*

Joel and Riley.

It would explain a whole heckuva lot.

"What type of horse do you have?" Joel asks.

"She's actually a Trakehner. Dapple gray. A *splendid* mare." I couldn't pass it up. Had to throw the word in there.

"Oh gosh, they are on the high-strung side. I think they can be on the dumb side, too. No. I prefer a good, old-fashioned Thoroughbred when it comes to the sport of eventing. So reliable. They are all heart."

Ears heating up to dark purple. So happy my hair is not pulled back. I smile oh-so-sweetly. "As you say, Thoroughbreds are *all* heart. Makes me question *their* intelligence, at least at times. I'm not sure what you've discovered in your experience, but I have been very pleased with my horse. I think she is a *splendid* breed." Okay, so it's a twinge of an exaggeration, but for the past few days, Harmony and I have been making some real strides together. For the record, I really don't think that Thoroughbreds are stupid.

"Yes, well, we all have our opinions," Joel replies as he dips his spoon into this ice thing that I am told by Riley's mother is to "cleanse the palate." Tastes like sherbet to me.

Joel and I are eyeing each other like two coiled snakes ready to strike when Mrs. Reed says, "Now you two children are aware that premarital sex is a sin?"

I choke a little on my steak.

"Yes, Mother," Riley quickly replies.

And it's on to dessert.


On the walk back to my dorm room, we are pretty quiet.

"Your folks are nice," I say, trying to make small talk.

"You don't have to lie, Vivvie. My folks aren't nice."

We walk a little farther.

"Riley? What's up with you and Joel?"

He stops walking, and so do I. The full moon illuminates his handsome face. The breeze coming off the Pacific carries with it that salty, clean ocean scent. If things weren't so tense, this would be a perfect night.

"You can't tell anyone," he says. "I have never told a soul. Please. You just can't. I am sorry I put you in this position. I really am. My dad kept asking me if I had met a girl I liked yet. Maybe he suspects. I don't know. Maybe he suspects that Joel and I . . . So I told him I liked you. That part is true." He looks down again. "Just not in that way," he clarifies. "If Joel transfers here, then everyone will know. My parents would probably put me in some kind of institution where a shrink or priest will try and convince me that I can be straight."

I take his hand. "I like you, too, Ri. You haven't put me in a bad position. Tonight was—well, it's what friends do for one another. And as far as Joel goes, let's cross that bridge when and *if* we have to." I hesitate, then blurt out, "What about Shannon? I heard you two were kind of hot and heavy, you know?"

He laughs. "Yeah, she was a good cover for a while. But she was always wanting *more*. I have to admit something to you that I'm not proud of, but when you came here I did see you as a way out from her, from that whole group. You seemed nice, kinda normal and cool. I figured making friends with you, I could seal my fate with them."

"Okay. And I kinda appreciate you being honest, but don't *ever* use me again." I shove him lightly, and we start laughing. "Jerk."

"Well, I won't deny it," he says. "So, we're cool?"

"Yeah, we're cool," I say.

Then . . . "There's more," Riley says.

"More?" He points to a bench next to the pond. I sit down.

"Yeah. More. And you aren't going to be happy about it."

I look up at him and speak before thinking. "Okay. Bring it."

CHAPTER *thirty-one*

e tells me about "the Bet."

"What?" I shriek, drowning out the night insects' serenade. I start to stand, and he grabs my hand.

"Please sit down. Please, Vivvie. I can explain! Please."

"Well then, you better start explaining. Now."

He tells me how the "scholarship girl initiation" works. "So . . . you are number one, Nate is two, and Tristan is three?"

"You got it."

"And you, you signed on because . . . because . . ." My heart was thudding so hard against my chest, and I couldn't help but let the anger continue to rise. "Let me guess why—wait, wait! Because you don't want anyone to know what I now know about you."

"Partly. Yes."

"You're such an ass."

"Please, just hear me out."

I cross my arms. "I am waiting for something to come of this that makes any sense to me on a friendship level."

"Okay. When I heard Joel was coming with my parents, that is when I agreed to get into the bet, but"—he holds up a hand before I can yell at him again—"I am telling you about it because I want to involve you."

"This is rich. Really rich, Ri. Do tell."

"I told you how I can't let my parents know about me—not now. And I am not stupid enough to think that I can go through life living a lie. I don't want to do that. Really, I don't."

He is so nervous and upset, I am having a hard time being as mad as I have every right to be. *Damn Riley.*

"But that doesn't mean you can just lie about me, and use me to—"

Riley flinches, but cuts me off. "Wait, here's the deal. After I graduate, I am going to go to Europe. I've been saving money for two years now. You know as well as I do that if I can get on at one of the big barns in the UK, my living and some schooling expenses will be paid for."

"How? How have you been saving money? Even if you are hired on as a working student, you'll need a decent sum to get by on."

"Poker. We have a not-so-on-the-up-and-up poker game in one of the guy's rooms every other Saturday night. I've won a lot. That money is going to provide for me that first year when I leave."

Then the lightbulb moment hits. "Wait. I get it. You want to win the money in this bet, and that is why you need me."

He nods.

I get up and start walking away.

He blocks me. "Listen, it's at eighteen thousand dollars right now. We can split it, Vivvie. Look, you know how you're always saying that you don't want a boyfriend and it'll interfere with your goals and blah, blah? Well, wouldn't people thinking you and I are hooking up get rid of that worry for you?"

I stop. There's *something* to what he's said. "What about Tristan? Did he accept his position as number three?"

Riley looks down before answering me. "Yes."

I shake my head. "Great. I'm in. I want half. And I get to be the one to orchestrates how this all goes down. Deal?"

"Vivienne Taylor, I will be your obedient servant." He gives me a peck on the cheek.

"I am still a little bit mad at you."

"I'm sorry."

"Good night, Riley."

"Night, Vivvie."

I decide that I don't want to go back to my room and be alone yet. Martina left me a voice mail while we were at dinner, saying that she's staying at her parents' house and will be back Sunday afternoon. I go down to visit Harmony.

It takes me a few seconds to locate the light switch in the dark barn. I hear horses shifting in their stalls, some still eating dinner, some walking in and out of their runs. I am greeted by a few at their stall doors, their curious eyes watching me.

Harmony stands in the darkened corner of her stall. "Hi, sweet girl." I take her face in my hands and look into her eyes. The light from outside the stall casts an eerie glow. I close my eyes to summon communication with her. "Can you tell me what happened to Serena? Do you know what happened to her? If you can tell me, then I think I can help you feel better." I show her a picture of a broken heart, and then I show the heart stitched up. "You'll miss her still . . ." I slide my palm down the front of her face, but she doesn't respond. "But I promise I can help make this better." I hope that what I'm telling her is the truth. Can I keep this promise?

The thought scares me that I might not be able to help her as much as I'm saying. But, I am compelled to discover what happened to Dr. Miller. I may not have known the woman personally, but I have been getting pieces of her through Harmony. This horse is such a good mare, and I know she is intelligent and sensitive. I have a strong sense that Serena cultivated those qualities in this horse.

Harmony suddenly shifts onto one of her hind legs and shows me an image of . . . her right eye. She is shrouded in a pitch-black darkness. Her face is turned to the side, and a hand is reaching out to touch it, but she pulls back, snorting as if scared. She is scared!

Then she shows me another other horse. The pretty bay again, and there's Lydia looking at the horse. Lydia is crying . . . Not just ordinary tears, but tears of blood!

Harmony's breathing is heavy, and I speak in hushed tones. "It's okay, good girl. Tell me. Tell me what you saw."

A stream of blood. Serena's face—distorted in pain but with dead eyes. A baseball cap is beside her, and a scorpion is crawling toward her face.

Then, total darkness.

I feel so dizzy. I slump against the stall wall and close my eyes, trying to breathe in steadily.

Harmony lowers her head next to me, her hot breath filtering down on me. I look up at her. "I'll find the truth. I will. I'll find out what happened to Serena for you. I promise."

CHAPTER *thirty-two*

I stay in my room all morning on Sunday. After last night and all of the emotions from Riley to Harmony, I kind of feel like I've been hit by a bus.

I focus on what I've discovered, learned, and been "told" by human and horse since my arrival at Fairmont. I open up a notebook and begin tapping my pencil.

So, what have I learned?

I have a traumatized horse who truly loved Serena. She is afraid of a bad man, baseball caps, and that jacket. Does the jacket Riley and I found at the Olympic House really belong to Holden? As far as I know, Riley still has it. I have to ask him. I call his cell, but it goes straight to voice mail. It's possible he is sleeping in, since it's Sunday morning and only eight o'clock.

But why would Holden want to hurt Dr. Miller, his own cousin? Really, she was more like a sister, since Holden's family had raised Serena since she was ten years old. But Martina said they didn't always get along. Why? Could their lukewarm relationship have been about sibling rivalry, since they'd been raised together? Speaking of relatives: there was that weirdo brother of Serena's who had been at her place when we went to pick up the blankets. He was all mad about her having a will. A will!

Did he push her off the ladder in anger over her will?

A new thought hits me. Christian Albright—the fiancé. Is he still in town? Serena had drawn up a will at his urging. He had gotten everything, according to him. *And* he had on a baseball cap the night I met him. Oh, God. What if he's a murderer? And what about that intimate embrace I saw between him and Kayla? And she'd been given Timmy *after* Serena died. Holden said that Timmy was finally the match that Kayla had been seeking in a horse.

These what-ifs are running rampant in my mind.

Then there is this element of Lydia Gallagher and a horse. I mean, seriously, what is that about?

I get up, go to the bookcase, and find last year's yearbook. As I flip through the pages I spot a photo of Lydia Gallagher with a horse whose name was Haute Couture. There is a RIP insignia in the caption. I suck back some air. Haute Couture is the horse in the image Harmony gave me out on the trail and then again last night.

What does it all mean?

I look at other photos, not really sure what I am looking for but hoping I might find something else.

And, I do.

Here is Dr. Miller. She was tall and thin, wore her blond hair pulled straight back. Pretty smile, nice eyes. She looks really happy in this photo. Her arm is wrapped around a student. The caption underneath the student reads: *Dr. Miller's Academy Assistant 2012.* Guess who it was?

*Oh my God.* Looks like I need to go make nice with one Emily Davenport.

CHAPTER *thirty-three*

I spend the next hour looking for Emily Davenport. Then I finally realize that it isn't just Emily I'm not seeing—the whole campus is practically deserted.

I ask one of the freshmen coming out of the cafeteria about this. "Oh yeah, a lot of kids went to the beach party. It's for kids whose parents are still here," the girl says.

What's a girl to do?

Today, the Indian summer heat is almost ninety and it's not even noon. I'm going to make lemonade out of lemons. Meaning, I am going to take advantage of the drop in population and take my white legs out in the sun and into the pool!

I rummage through my drawers and find my bathing suit tucked underneath a few pairs of breeches. I put on a T-shirt and a pair of shorts over it and make my way to the pool. There are only a hand-ful of freshman hanging out. I've discovered that with the freshmen and even some sophomores, being the scholarship kid is considered pretty cool. They apparently have not received the memo from the DZ and Lydia. A few of them even say hey as I walk past.

I find a lounge chair, face it toward the sun, spread out a towel, and plop down on it. Ah, yes. Perfect. I slather myself with sunscreen because even though I want a tan, I know the color that my skin will turn is cherry red. At least, with some sunscreen I might get a little color. Okay, at least I'd get some Vitamin D. And hopefully a nap.

I've brought down some homework with me. Boring, but necessary. I need to read over the "marketing strategy" that Tristan has created for "Goode & Taylor Farms." He e-mailed it to me so we could go over it on Wednesday during our study session. Just seeing his name on the paper makes my stomach sink. But is it sinking in that *oh, I can't wait to see him* way? Or in that *I am dreading seeing him* way? The latter would be far more appropriate, but the former is, pathetically, probably more accurate. If I were to explore my feelings, which I do not want to do, then I am pretty sure it's a combination of the two. Which is the stronger feeling is what I'm not sure about. I can't even believe that I'm thinking this way. The guy is a jerk. An ass. A total jerk! A delicious total jerk. Yeah, I hate him.

I am curious, though, about his plan. What has he come up with?

I start to read over it. Damn, it's actually good. He writes that marketing "our barn" at various events, through social media and regional advertising, and by hosting a first-class clinic will bring in the right type of clients we are seeking—for *our barn*. I know. I totally know that this is all pretend and for a class project, but there is this little part of me getting kind of wrapped up in the fantasy of it all.

Then . . . specifics—on us. On me, to be exact. My ears burn.

*Gold Medal Olympian Vivienne Taylor, partner in Goode & Taylor, will be hosting the clinic.* My stomach does that thing again.

It goes on: *Ms. Taylor's gold medal adds to the promotional appeal of the barn. It is additionally beneficial that Ms. Taylor is highly knowledgeable both as a horsewoman and businessperson. She is able to offer a critical eye without making a rider feel discouraged. She's also attractive, which can be a benefit when dealing with the public, as studies have shown that good-looking people tend to be more successful.*

I throw the paper down and ball up my fists. What the hell is this guy trying to do! *This* is his *big move*—to win the bet! Does he really believe that because he compliments me in some stupid paper, that I will throw my panties at him? On top of it, that statement about attractiveness and success comes off as pretentious to me.

I shove the paper back into my bag and think of as many mean comebacks as possible. One thing for sure is that come Monday morning I'm heading straight to Mr. Bromley's office to request a new partner.

But for now, I strip off my shorts, dive in the pool, and swim several furious laps. Finally cooled down, both literally and figuratively, I climb out totally ready for that nap I've been yearning for.

The warm sun on my back relaxes me, and a sense of warmth and peace and darkness passes through me. I begin to dream.

*There's Dean, and he's cantering through the field on the back side of our house. His tail sails behind him. He bucks and plays and then stops.*

*He snorts and tosses his head high. He then takes off again down the fence line. Another horse comes into view. It's Harmony!*

*Harmony trots up to Dean and nuzzles him.*

*Then a dense fog rolls in, and both horses vanish from my sight.*

*Now I'm now in Serena's barn, standing over her broken body. I hear whinnies from the other stalls. I see a falling ladder coming toward me. I jump out of the way, and hear the crash as it hits the ground.*

*Someone walks past Serena, who is on the ground, dead. It is someone wearing a baseball cap, but I can't see who it is. A fog begins to thicken around me till it's everywhere and all I can see.*

*I feel warm hands rubbing my back. Mmmm. That's nice.*

Then I feel the string on my bikini top being tugged on slightly, tickling me. It's nice, too—the feeling of it travels through me.

"You're getting sunburned. Thought you might need some sunscreen," someone whispers in my ear.

I flip over, holding on to my top. "What the hell are you doing?"

Tristan holds out his hands, palms open. "Sorry. I saw you were getting sunburned, and I thought maybe you needed some protection. I didn't mean to startle you."

"I don't need any *protection*! Thank you. What were you doing with my top?"

He shakes his head and smiles. "Nothing. I swear. I was just moving the strings out of the way. That's all."

I stare at him, my eyes squinting into slits of anger. "Really? Really! I heard all about your little bet."

"What?"

"The scholarship girl initiation. I know all about it!"

Tristan actually turns red. "Oh God. Look, I told Nate it was stupid. I did. I did not take the bet. I would never do that!"

"Right. Well, good. We're on the same page, because you're not ever getting this. Ever."

The shade of red on his face deepens. "I'm sorry. I never—"

I hold up my hand and throw my things in my bag. "That's right—you will never! I see how hard you try to convince yourself that you're really not like the rest of your little group. That you're a good guy who just happens to have the biggest bitch here as your girlfriend, because why? Because she's so nice and smart and funny? No! If you really are who you tried so hard to make me believe you are, the other day when you asked me if I was at all interested in you, then you'd break up with Lydia!"

He bows his head.

"You don't understand why I haven't broken up with Lydia, but it's not what you think!"

"I think . . . I think . . . what I *think* is that I honestly don't care!" I grab my things and storm off, tears blurring my vision.

CHAPTER *thirty-four*

Tristan pretty much wants to slam Nate Deacon up against a wall and beat his ass. But what good will that do? He's screwed. And he's done it to himself.

He goes to see Sebastian in order to try to cool down. If there is a being on this planet that can soothe him in this moment, it's the horse that has been his trusted friend since he was twelve years old. His dad has never understood his relationship with Sebastian. Sports and money. That's what his father understands about horses. That's it. If he was different, he could never have done the cruel things Tristan knows about—could he?

In Sebastian's stall, the horse rubs his face on Tristan's chest. Tristan buries his face in his horse's neck.

"I'm so stuck," he whispers.

Vivienne. She is so different from Lydia and the girls he hangs out with. She's sensitive and smart, and he has ruined any chance he might ever have with her.

If only that night hadn't happened. The eighth of July.

His father had some of his business partners over to watch one of the horse races on TV. One of the slew of horses his dad owns was racing.

Tristan never liked his father's partners. They were loud and crude, most of them always drunk. There was something hard and I-don't-give-a-shit about these guys. They were also a little scary.

His mom had locked herself in her room. Her signature move.

Tristan's dad had ordered him to pour this guy a glass of gin or that guy some bourbon. They were all getting tanked.

The house staff had a day off. Afterward, Tristan wondered if that had been planned.

The horse that belonged to his dad and his partners lost the race. Poor colt came in seventh.

As the men grew drunker, Tristan overheard their plan. Feeling shaky and sick to his stomach, he swiped a bottle of tequila and did some shots in his room. They burned and went straight to his head.

And he called Lydia.

"Tristan! Hi, baby. How are you?"

"I don't know." He could hear a tremor in his voice.

"What do you mean? You sound strange. What's wrong?"

"It's my dad," he'd blurted out. "And these guys he does business with. They're going to . . ."

"Going to what?"

"They're going to kill at least one of the racehorses they own, maybe more, so they can collect the insurance money," he whispered into the phone.

"What? What did you say?"

"They're going to kill a horse for the money, Lydia. The insurance money, and it sounded to me like this was not the first time, and it won't be the last."

"Oh my God. What are you going to do?" she asked.

"I don't know." He'd closed his eyes and laid flat on his bed, the ceiling swirling.

"You have to tell someone."

"I can't. He's my dad."

"But it's so wrong."

"Of course, it's wrong," Tristan hissed. "But these guys that he deals with are not good people. I think they could be, like, Mafia. They're definitely criminals."

"Tell your mom. You have to."

"No. I can't tell her. She could never handle it. And you can't tell anyone either. *Promise me. Please.* You can't tell anyone. *Ever.* If you do, I'll never be allowed back at school."

"Okay. I promise," she said. "But why can't you at least talk to your mother? Maybe she can help."

And that is when he told her about his mother, nailing the final nail in his coffin where Lydia was concerned. She *had* him.

A week later Tristan learned that the colt that had lost the race had died from a heart attack during the morning workout. He went to his father.

"I know what you and your partners did to that colt!" he yelled. His father sat at the breakfast table serenely drinking his morning coffee, eating a piece of toast, and reading the newspaper.

"You do, huh?" The son of a bitch did not even look up from the paper.

"Yeah, I do, and it's sick, and cruel, and wrong. And I am going to report you! I heard *everything* you guys planned."

Mr. Goode had set down the newspaper calmly and looked at Tristan. "You know, son, that would be a very, very dumb thing to do. I could go to jail. You'd be stuck here with Mom. No more Fairmont. No more Sebastian."

"I'm willing to risk that." His mother had her own money. He could bring Sebastian home and board him at a local facility.

"You willing to risk a *life*, Tristan?" His father slammed his fist down on the table. "You willing to risk the life of that damn *horse* you love so much?" He looked at him with dark, furious eyes.

"What do you mean?"

"Just that, son. You go and report what you heard, the men I deal with have enough money, good lawyers . . . they'll be out of jail, if they even go, in no time. But your horse, he might just wind up dead."

That had been the end of their conversation, and so much more. And if Lydia ever tells a soul . . .

CHAPTER *thirty-five*

artina is in our room when I get back. She looks upset, so I decide not to add my personal drama to what might be going on with her.

"Hey," she says. "How's it going?"

"Pretty good. I was just out at the pool. How are your folks?" I plop down on my bed.

"They're doing okay, I guess. This stalker thing has my dad really frazzled. And my mom is kind of blowing the whole thing off."

"What do *you* think? I mean, how do you feel?"

I see her shoulders tense. "My dad worries a lot, and my mom is kind of this carefree spirit who always thinks the best of people. Between the two of them, I really don't know what to think. But both of them insist I should not worry about it and just do my thing here. Go to school, and all that . . ." She smiles, but it doesn't quite reach her eyes. "Anything new and interesting happen around here while I was gone?"

Now, there's a loaded question. I think I'll steer clear of the Tristan debacle, and I can't say anything about Riley. Can't talk about Harmony either. Huh. "There was one weird thing."

"Oh yeah? What was that?"

"Yesterday at Parents' Day, I took a walk down to the fountain, and I ran into Lydia Gallagher and her brother Daniel. He's kind of strange. I thought it was also strange that I didn't see their parents with them. Then, the brother—Daniel—brought you up. Said to tell Tina 'hi.' I corrected him, though, and reminded him that your name is Martina. Guy seems every bit of the jerk that his sister is."

Martina doesn't say anything. When I look over at her, she turns away. *Uh-oh.* "Martina? You okay?"

"He is every bit the jerk his sister is and then some." She glances out the window, and when she looks back my way I can see the beginning of tears in her eyes.

"Do you want to talk about it?"

She sighs. "You'll hear about it soon enough, I'm sure. Lydia likes to make sure she churns the rumor mill up now and again with past gossip."

"What happened?"

"When I was a freshman—when Lydia and I and the rest of her groupies were freshmen—Daniel was a senior here. He was actually on the Young Equestrian team, and just like Tristan Goode, he was the guy that every girl was madly in love with."

My face burns at the mention of Tristan's name.

"I had a huge crush on Daniel. From day one, Lydia had it in for me because she knew who my parents were. Apparently when she was a little kid she had tried to do some acting. She was even cast in a movie that my dad was working on. Something happened, and she claims he was the reason she was let go from the movie."

"He fired her?"

"Technically, yes. As you can imagine, she was a bit of a spoiled brat."

"Impossible!" We both laugh, which lightens the mood some.

"Yeah. Pretty crazy that we both end up at Fairmont. And she somehow figures out who my parents are. Then she catches wind that I am crushing on her big brother, so she sets it up with him to ask me out. Viv, he was really sweet to me, and I thought he really liked me." She shakes her head. "Then he started pressuring me to have sex with him."

"Did you?"

"No. But everyone *thinks* I did. Lydia snuck into my room and took a pair of panties and a bra of mine and put it in his room. She took pictures and texted them to anyone and everyone she knew."

"Why didn't she get suspended or expelled?"

"Never been able to prove it, but I know it was her. Then, a few days later, in front of a group of kids, Daniel calls me a slut and tells me that he never really liked me—that girls *like me* are only good for one thing." She swipes at some tears.

I stand up, walk over, and wrap my arms around my friend. "I am so sorry. That is horrible. We will get even. I promise."

"No. It's in the past. I just want to leave it there."

"But Lydia will never let you."

"True."

"What's her deal? I mean, where are their parents?"

"Who knows? I've heard that Daniel runs almost everything and that their parents are always vacationing and doing whatever they do. I know he runs the equestrian end of things. He helped Lydia buy her new horse after her mare, Haute Couture, died last year. He flies out here to watch her at all of the major events. I think I've only seen her mom one time."

"Wow. How did her mare die?"

"Kidney failure."

"Really? That's kind of rare."

"I'd heard that she had some kidney issues previously, a couple of years ago. I guess like people, some horses just get sick."

"Sad, but true. You know what we need?" I smile.

"What?"

"No more downer discussion."

"I'm with you on that," she agrees. "Oh! I know what you're thinking now."

I walk into the front room of our suite and put in the new Taylor Swift CD that neither one of us seems to be getting remotely sick of. "Dance party?" I yell.

She comes into the front room. "A little 'feeling twenty-two'?" she asks.

"Yep."

The two of us dance like crazy fools, both hoping to rid ourselves for the moment of old gossip, new rumors, or simply unnecessary ugliness.

CHAPTER *thirty-six*

This week is going by pretty much in a blur for me. I haven't gotten anything new from Harmony or been able to get Emily Davenport in a solo moment. Harmony is repeating the same images to me, but like me, I think she has switched to competition mode. Our first event is only two days away. Recent lessons have been intense and driven.

Riley and I have now kind of gotten into this bet. He tells me that the betting pool is at twenty-two grand! It's weird to me that Tristan hasn't spilled about my knowing what's up. He barely looks at me in barn management class, in which, by the way, Mr. Bromley did not allow me to switch partners. I sent Tristan an e-mail letting him know that e-mails were the only way we would be working on the assignment together.

And as far as Nate Deacon is concerned? Well . . . trust me, he is going to get what he deserves.

After barn management class that morning, I catch up with him in the hall. "Hey, Nate."

"Hey, Red."

"I hear you have a little poker game going this Thursday." Riley told me that since the event is happening Friday and Saturday, the guys moved their game date up.

Nate cocks his head to the side, probably thinking it makes him look like a vulnerable and cute little puppy dog. I only see a mongrel. "You did?"

"I did, and I have a proposition for you."

"I like the sound of *that*."

"I thought you might. How about you letting me join in?"

"Oh no, Red. No chicks allowed."

I frown. "Oh, c'mon. Please. I've always wanted to learn how to play. And who knows? I might have a little surprise for you afterward if you invite me."

He looks me up and down and then eyes me. "Really? Is it one I might like?"

"Possibly. Let's just say that it might involve my panties."

"Okay then, Red, yeah, I would be interested in *that*. You have an official invite."

I am in a pretty good mood the rest of the day. My jump lesson with Newman goes exceptionally well, and Harmony eagerly takes extra treats from me. "You ready for this weekend, girl?" I stroke her neck. As I'm talking to my mare, I hear something. Someone is crying.

It's coming from the tack room. I walk over and see a girl sitting on her tack trunk. "Emily?"

She looks up at me with tear-stained eyes. "Go away, Scholarship."

"Hey, you know, I'm not that bad."

"Right. Whatever."

"Look, I don't mean to pry. But if I had to guess why you're so upset, I'd say it has something to do with your mother."

She doesn't say anything.

"You know, I've heard the way she is with you, and she's . . . wrong." I take a step farther into the tack room.

"What do you mean?" she asks.

"She's just—she's wrong about you and your skills. You are an excellent rider. You really are. I have to tell you, though, that it doesn't look like you enjoy it very much."

Several long seconds tick by.

Finally, she says, "I *don't* like it. I don't like riding."

"Then why are you here?"

"It's my *mother's* thing. I used to like it. When I was a little kid there was nothing I wanted to do more than ride my own horse. But then she got all involved and ruined everything." She sighs. "She thinks she knows everything because she teaches some backyard lessons out near our house, which she only does because she's so bored with her stupid life."

"That doesn't sound too good." I have no idea what to say here.

"The other thing she does when she's bored is pick on me. 'Emily, you didn't have your heels down. Emily, what was wrong with your horse? Emily, why can't you ride like Lydia? Oh, and she's even thrown you in there now. Emily, look at the new girl. Why can't you ride like her?'"

"That sucks. I'm sorry." I sit down on the tack trunk beside her. "I really am."

"I love horses. But I hate riding. I want to become a vet."

"My mom's a vet."

"Really?" Her tone actually changes from sullen to sort of interested.

"Yeah. I used to go out with her on calls. I miss that."

She hangs her head. "I used to go out on calls sometimes with Dr. Miller."

"She sounds like she was a really nice woman."

Emily chokes back a sob. "She was. I used to wish she was my mom. I can't believe she's gone."

"You two were close?"

"I was her student assistant last year. She was nice to me, and real. Just totally down to earth."

I don't want to ask, but what was her reference to the *real* part? Was she implying something about her *unreal* friends?

If I am going to ask her what I want, or think I might need, it has to be now. I take a deep breath. "I know I am taking a chance here by even asking you, and I am positive you will run off and go blab to Lydia, but this is something I need to do."

"I don't know what you're talking about," she says.

"I don't think that Dr. Miller's accident was an accident."

"What?" The color in Emily's face drains.

"I think she was murdered, and I think that whatever happened to Lydia Gallagher's horse Haute Couture last year had something to do with it."

Emily doesn't say a word. So I continue. "I think Dr. Miller knew what happened to that horse."

"It was kidney failure," Emily insists, but I can hear something in her voice.

"Emily, if you did some work with Dr. Miller, then you have to know what I know about horses' kidneys. Renal failure is not common. Is it possible there's something more to it? Do you know if she did a necropsy on the horse?"

She looks away.

"If Dr. Miller did a necropsy, what if she found something that would implicate someone associated with the horse?"

"Where did you hear this?" Emily whispers, her voice shaking.

"I just did. I need to find out if what I heard was true."

"What do you want from me?"

I can see that her eyes are filled with tears again, and she won't look directly at me.

"Emily, do you have access to Serena's computer? Her files, anything like that?"

"I have to go," she says. "I'm sorry, Scholarship. I can't help you."

Emily walks out the aisleway, and I turn to see Lydia, hands on hips, waiting for her at the barn's entrance. I've spooked Emily for sure. I am also sure she knows something about what really happened to Lydia's horse and to Serena. The thing I am most certain of here is what I recognized in Emily's eyes—cold fear. What she is afraid of, I don't know. But I am positive that Emily Davenport is scared to death.

# RILEY

## CHAPTER *thirty-seven*

R iley is nervous. First off, he hates putting Vivvie in this position, even though she insisted on it. Secondly, he has lied to her about Tristan's involvement in the bet. But he has his reasons. He knows they are totally selfish, but Vivienne did say that she did not want a boyfriend, so he's taken Tristan off the table for her. Is that really so bad? Besides, as much as he likes Tristan, he doesn't think the guy would be good at all for Vivvie.

Riley grabs his sweater and backpack and heads out to Nate's room, where tonight's poker game—and a few other festivities—are about to go down.

When he arrives, there is all the usual high-fiving and slaps on the back.

"You ready for tonight, Reed?" Nate asks.

Riley rubs his hands together. "Gentlemen, I am going to kick every ass in this place."

"Keep believing your delusions, brother. Keep on believing

them. Hey, just so you know, Red says she wants in tonight. Says she has a surprise for me afterwards. Told you that I wasn't out of this game yet."

"Oh yeah?"

The room is filling up. Six of the seven usual suspects are now present.

"Yeah, man. I think she got bored waiting around for you to make a move, and Tristan is too hung up on Lydia. You hitting that yet, brother?" He slaps Tristan hard on the shoulder. Riley notices his pal cringe.

"I told you I wasn't in on that thing. I'm surprised you are, Ri," Tristan says. "What changed your mind?"

"The money, man!" Nate laughs. "Plus, that girl is hhhhotttt."

Tristan had told both Nate and Riley that he wasn't going to be involved. He couldn't blame Riley for being mad and disappointed with him. "I guess we'll see, Nate. Let the best man win."

"That's right, Reed. The best man *is* going to win. Wonder where Red is? I say we get started. She'll show soon."

Riley deals the first round, and the game is on.

An hour passes, and Riley notices that Nate keeps checking his watch.

Finally, about an hour and a half into the game, there's a knock at the door. Nate jumps up so fast that he knocks over his chair. When he opens the door, there stands Vivienne, still in her riding clothes.

Nate smiles, looking creepily like the joker. "Glad you could make it, Red. Me and the boys were beginning to wonder."

"Oh. Sorry I'm late. And that I didn't change." She shoots Riley a quick look and lets out an exaggerated sigh. "I had this really cute skirt I wanted to wear, but you know what? I had a problem."

"You did?" Nate asks.

"You see, I have a lucky pair of panties."

Low chuckles spread out through the group.

"You do?"

"Mm-hmm. I wear them when I get lucky. I figured that tonight I wanted to get lucky, but I couldn't find them. So I started thinking, now where could I have left my lucky panties?"

More immature chuckles. Only Tristan is silent, staring down at the table. Riley knows his face is deep red, and Nate looks like he is about to burst out of his skin.

"Then I remembered. Riley? Do you have something of mine?"

"I th—think I do," he stammers.

"From the other night? In the tack room?"

Riley nods.

"Well, can I have them back? I mean, when we almost got caught by Kayla, you shoved them in your backpack. Are they still there?"

Riley picks his backpack up off the floor and unzips it. He takes out the light pink lacy panties she gave him earlier that day. Now, it's hoot and whistles from the peanut gallery.

"There they are. My lucky panties. For poker, three-day events, anything I want to get lucky for. They are a must." She walks over and gives Riley a kiss on the lips. "Thank you." She winks at him. "Now boys, I do believe you all owe *my boyfriend* some money. I'd love to sit down and play with you, but I don't want to shake up the game at this point. Plus, I want to go over my dressage test again for tomorrow. See you later." She holds the panties on her finger and twirls them as she walks out.

The room is now silent.

When the door closes behind her, everyone looks at Riley. "Riley, you and Vivienne?" Tristan asks, not trusting his voice.

Riley nods.

"Well, then, I guess everyone needs to pay the man," Tristan says.

They all hand over the cash they'd put into the pool—twenty-two thousand, six hundred dollars.

After Riley puts the cash away, Tristan stands up and tosses in his chips. "I'm out. I'm tired, and I want to look at my test again, too."

Riley watches Tristan leave. He *should* feel good about the money. He is that much closer to his goal of freedom. But he doesn't feel good. He feels like a complete ass.

CHAPTER *thirty-eight*

It's the morning after the poker game, and I wake up exhausted from visions of pink panties, drooling guys, sick horses, baseball caps, falling ladders, dead hands, blood, and a scorpion invading my dreams and my life.

At 5:45 a.m. Martina and I go to the cafeteria for our morning cup of coffee and to meet up with Riley. While Martina is at the counter doctoring her coffee, I whisper to Riley, "What happened after I left?"

"Actually, you kind of brought the game to a standstill. Tristan folded, said he wanted to go back over his dressage test. Then I did the same thing—after I collected our cash."

"He knows today's test perfectly. I've been watch—"

"Watching him." Riley finishes my sentence.

"Yeah," I utter in total shame.

"I know you like the guy, Vivvie."

"Riley, I *cannot* like him. I mean, he was involved in that stupid bet, *and* he has a girlfriend. He's just . . . Tristan's a distraction.

And like I told you, I came here to achieve certain goals. Not be distracted."

He nods. "I want to talk to you about all that."

"About what?" I take a sip from my coffee.

Martina comes up to us. "Should we go down to the barn?" she asks.

"Yep." We pick up our show clothes, bagged and ready. Dressage will run all morning, and stadium will take up the afternoon.

I am competing Harmony at the preliminary level. My competition is Lydia, Tristan, Emily, Riley, Shannon, and Martina.

Our dressage test time is 11:08. After Harmony finishes her breakfast, I take her out of her stall. As I'm braiding her mane she repeatedly shows me Serena and Christian, who's wearing *the* cap. They are arguing, and I can feel anger between them. Then she shows Serena walking away from Christian, and I feel a surge of sadness—from Harmony? Serena? Christian? Both? I'm just not sure.

Then Harmony shows me Christian opening his hand. In it is a diamond ring—did Serena call off their engagement? Or maybe this is just before he proposed? He might even have proposed in the barn.

As I'm wrapping the last braid, Holden walks into the barn. "Hey, Vivienne. You ready for today?"

"I hope so."

"You're going to be great. You've been working hard, and this horse, she has been trying for you. I can see it."

I smile. "Thank you." I can't help but feel somewhat awkward around Holden, thinking that Kayla could possibly be cheating on him.

"Okay. I want you in the warm-up in thirty," Holden says.

"You got it." I finish grooming Harmony, and change into my show clothes. My mom spent an ungodly amount buying me a new dressage coat, white breeches, beige breeches, a hunt coat, and an air vest for cross-country. My half of the bet money is in some way going back to my mom. I just can't let her know how I got it. I'll have to be *creative* with my well-earned windfall.

I've got my show clothes on, Harmony is tacked up, and our warm-up is going smoothly. We are in sync, and this is the best I've felt since coming to Fairmont.

Holden calls me over. "Walk her out. You're on deck after Lydia."

I try to maintain calm and not transfer any nervous energy into Harmony as I run through the test in my head.

I watch as Lydia and Geisha perform. They do amazingly well, as close to perfect as anyone could possibly be.

Now Harmony and I are trotting around the arena. The bell chimes and we enter the ring.

A: Enter working trot.

X: Halt salute

C: Track right

Each movement goes through my head automatically. I have done this test in the arena, in my head, and even in my sleep. And as we work through each gait, each movement in precision together, my mind is concentrating, my heart is beating, a connection is happening between Harmony and me that melds us.

Seventeenth movement working trot at C.

Turn right at B.

At X turn right, and finally at G, halt and salute.

As we salute, I hear the applause. I pat Harmony on both sides of her neck as I allow her to walk out of the arena on a long rein. I am so happy! She has been absolutely spectacular. The quality of the trot, her transitions, her counter canter, her balance—all of it.

We come out of the arena, and there's Tristan off to the side. He smiles and gives me a thumbs-up. I can't help it. I smile back. Riley is standing next to him. He salutes us, then inclines his head to the side, indicating that he needs to go get on Santos.

Kayla and Holden come up to me, hand in hand. "Good job, Vivienne. You should be happy with that," Kayla says.

"I am. I really am."

"Still have two more events to go," Holden pointlessly reminds me. "Keep at it. Better get her taken care of, so you can be ready this afternoon for stadium. Don't you go at two twelve?"

"I do."

"Newman will want you in the warm-up, then, at one forty. Make sure you have some lunch."

I take Harmony back to the barn, remove her dressage tack, brush her down, and give her a snack. When I come out of the tack room, I am face to face with Lydia. "Excellent ride," I say.

"It was."

"Right. Must have been difficult, though. Isn't this the first event on your new horse? I heard about what happened to Haute Couture."

She crosses her arms in front of her. "It was very difficult. I loved her. But I am fortunate to have found Geisha now."

"To replace Haute." I cross my arms, too.

"No. I could never replace her. You can't just replace an animal you've loved. I'm not like that."

I study her, more than a little surprised. "Of course. It's horrible how she died."

"Why do you care so much about how my horse died?"

"Oh, it's just that my mom is a large-animal vet. So I know that renal failure is pretty rare. I'm curious as to what the issues were. I may be going into veterinary medicine myself."

"Haute had kidney issues. Period. Are you really interested from a veterinary medicine point of view? What are you really getting at, Scholarship?"

What was I getting at, exactly? "I'm not getting at *anything*, other than I think it's odd how Dr. Miller died so soon after your horse."

"So?"

"Right. So . . . so, I have to go to lunch. See you at stadium."

As I start to walk out of the barn, feeling piercing daggers on my back, I run into none other than Christian Albright. "Hello, Vivienne."

"Oh, hello. Hey, I was wondering . . . ," I start to say when he holds up his hand.

"Hate to cut you off, but I see Lydia down there, and I need to speak with her. Can we talk later?"

"Sure."

Goose bumps snake down my spine as several ugly thoughts enter my head. What if Christian Albright pushed Serena off that ladder? What if Lydia knew about it? Was Lydia's horse connected somehow? And, honestly, I'm not sure any of this is right on. But I can't help feeling like I'm getting closer to solving what really happened to Serena.

CHAPTER *thirty-nine*

Our stadium round is double clear and by the end of the day, guess where we are in the standings? First! Yes, Harmony and I are in first place, with Lydia on our heels in second, then Riley, which I am extremely happy about. We are followed by Shannon, Tristan, Martina, and finally Emily—who has been aggressively avoiding me.

When I fall into bed that night I slip fast into a dream-free sleep. But when I wake up at around five, my stomach is killing me. Is it nerves? It has to be nerves. I love cross-country. Though there is some pressure to it all, I know Harmony and I can handle it. Plus, I want to kick Lydia's butt.

Then an image of Harmony comes to mind. She is down in her stall, on the ground, thrashing. I put on my shoes, don't even change out of my pajamas, and book it as fast as I can down to the barn.

There she is, totally down inside her stall! On the wall next to the barn's office is an emergency phone that dials directly to Kayla and Holden.

I pick up the phone, my hands shaking. *Must get her up, get a vet*—-Kayla picks up on the third ring. "It's Vivienne. Harmony is down. I think she's colicking. Please call the vet!"

"Okay, honey. We'll be right down. Can you get her up?"

"I'm going to try," I say, trying to keep focused, not fall apart the way I want to.

I rush into her stall and lean down over her. Her eyes are wide with pain. I place a hand on her neck. "It's okay, big girl. It's going to be okay. I need you to try and get up."

She shows me her food.

"I know. I know it's stuck, but the vet is on the way and I promise you're going to be okay. Can you stand up for me? Can you?" When a horse colics, keeping them on their feet is vital so they don't roll and twist their intestines. The thing is, I don't know how long she's been down, and if she's been rolling. I swallow back the lump in my throat.

I gently nudge her, and she must finally trust me, because she stands up, though very shakily. *God, please let her be okay.*

Kayla and Holden arrive. Holden goes into the office, immediately gets a syringe of Banamine, and injects her with the med.

"Let's get her walking," Kayla says. "Try to get her over on the green grass. See if she'll eat some."

I guide her slowly over to a small grassy patch outside the barn. She puts her head down to the grass, takes a meager nibble, and that's it. This is so not good. I am really scared.

Fifteen long minutes pass before the vet shows up. Meanwhile, the campus is starting to come to life as students arrive to feed, add water, and clean stalls.

"Vivienne, this is Dr. Lawson," Kayla says, introducing me to a young, dark-haired woman.

"Hi. Let's see what's going on with your mare, Vivienne." I like how she gets right down to business.

Dr. Lawson does an extensive exam, and then tells me what I already know. "She's colicking. I don't think we are looking at surgery, but I cannot rule it out."

"We already gave her Banamine," Kayla lets her know.

"Good. Okay, I'm going to give her a little sedation and oil her. Get some electrolytes going, too."

I am the daughter of a vet. I don't get squeamish when needles have to be used. It doesn't bother me when the vet has to guide the tube for oiling a horse up through the nostril and down through the trachea and into the gastrointestinal tract. It doesn't. But for some reason, this time, with this horse—it does.

I can feel Harmony's distress and panic even with the sedation she's been given. As Dr. Lawson begins to pump the oil into her to lubricate the digestive tract and help any foods that have gotten stuck pass out of her, Harmony gives me an image of a hand and leaves. Then she shows me the bucket of oats, beet pulp, and carrots that she is fed every day. The hand, the leaves—it's all a little confusing.

A little over an hour later, Dr. Lawson is packing up. "Now, we wait and see. I think we caught it early enough. To me, she is already looking a bit more bright-eyed. I'll stop back by late this afternoon. If you see anything that looks like she is going into distress again, call immediately. No feed for her today. Maybe if she passes the oil by the time I see her this afternoon, you can mix her up a bran mash, but nothing else. Let's see how it goes for now." She shakes my hand and says her good-byes to the Fairmonts.

Kayla puts an arm around me. "I am so sorry, Vivienne. You two were doing so well in this event, and—"

I smile through my tears. "I don't care about the event. I just want to make sure she gets through this."

"Of course. I'll be sure and scratch you," Kayla promises.

"Thanks."

"Why don't we have Martina bring you down some clothes, and maybe some food?" Holden asks. "I have a feeling you won't be leaving her today." He places a hand on my shoulder. "She's going to be okay."

I nod, but can't say anything.

Throughout the day, I hear the loudspeaker echoing with Holden's voice announcing horse after horse as each goes out on cross-country. Gradually, Harmony does seem to be feeling better. When Dr. Lawson comes back by late in the afternoon as promised, Harmony has begun passing the oil. I mix her up a bucket of wheat bran and warm water to help the process along.

As the evening comes on, music floats in from the park where the barbecue is taking place. Soon after, Riley shows up with a plate of food. "Hey, you," he says.

"Hey, yourself."

"Kayla says she's doing better."

"Seems to be."

He hands me the plate.

I step out of the stall, and we go into the tack room and sit down on the trunks. I mix around the potato salad on my plate. I finally ask, "Well?"

"Lydia won."

"Thought so."

"I came in a respectable second." He smiles.

I high-five him. "Right on!" Then I start eating.

"Martina?"

"Fourth."

"Awesome!"

"Shannon was, I think, sixth; Emily was fifth."

"Good for her."

"You haven't asked about Tristan."

"Nope."

"Third."

"Oh."

"I have to tell you something, Vivvie."

"Two questions first: Will it be complicated, and will I wind up mad at you?"

"Yes, and probably."

I laugh. "Go ahead, clear your conscience."

Riley fidgets. "Tristan was *not* involved in the bet—not at all. He told Nate it was stupid and he wanted no part of it."

I set down my pulled pork sandwich and just stare at him. "So why did you lie to me and say he was a part of it? Really, I said some truly horrible things to him."

"I . . . look, you said yourself that you aren't here to go out with anyone, and—and there's this way he looks at you, and I know you're hot for him, too."

"Wait a minute, he does not and *I* am not—but even if he was and I was, why would you care?"

"Because, if you and Tristan were to hook up, then you and I— and I don't mean just this farce we have going as a couple, but I mean as friends, well . . . I know how these things go. Before long your lunches, dinners, study hall, would be with him, and not me."

"First off, I'm not one of those girls who just tosses away her friends when she gets a boyfriend. Okay, I've never had a real boyfriend. But I'm still not that girl, and you should already know that about me. Next, I also don't lie to friends, and I don't trust people who lie to me. You know what, Riley? I want you to go. I'm going to go spend some time alone with my horse."

As he walks out of the tack room, he turns around and says, "I am so sorry."

And I say, "I so wish that was enough."

CHAPTER *forty*

When Tristan knocks on Lydia's door, she opens it and immediately wraps her arms around his neck. "Today was incredible, wasn't it?"

*See the incredible dead man walking.*

Most guys would kill for a girl who looks like Lydia, but for him it is all about Vivienne. He knew she must be so anxious about Harmony's colicking, and, less noble truth to tell, he can't get those pink panties banished from his mind. Not to mention how he'd felt about her and Riley . . . until he'd found out . . .

After the barbecue, he'd taken a shower and got dressed to take Lydia out to a movie to celebrate her win. She wanted dinner, but he maneuvered her into agreeing to see a movie instead. Just as he was about to leave, Riley came in, head down and looking like he'd just lost his last friend.

When Riley told him what was going on, Tristan said, "Why are you telling me all this, Ri?"

"Because," Riley said, "I am sick of lying to people I care about. I hurt Vivienne by lying to her, and I hope that we can still be friends, T."

"We are, man. I don't care if you're gay. I don't. You're a good guy. I've always told you that." Tristan promised not to say anything to anyone. Everyone has something they don't want anyone to know about. *God knows I am no exception.*

But the information that Riley shared doesn't free Tristan from being stuck in Lydia's snare. Still, he is absurdly happy that Vivienne and Riley haven't hooked up.

"We are good together, Tristan. We look good together. I am sooo happy we are *together!*"

Lydia rubs his back and tilts her face up. He knows she wants him to kiss her. Tristan closes his eyes, imagines Vivienne in front of him, and goes through with it.

"Mmm . . . I like that," she says. "Why don't we head into town for that movie? I just need to put some makeup on."

"You look fine."

"Oh, Tristan. Please. Give me a few. You know, why don't we invite Riley and Vivienne? I really feel bad about her horse, and you're right, I guess I have been kind of a bitch to her, but really I was just sort of, breaking her in." She walks off toward the bathroom.

"I don't know—how about if tonight it's just us?" He doesn't think he could handle being next to Vivienne at a movie and not be with her. Plus, he's sure she wouldn't accept an invite anyway.

"Fabulous. Whatever you want."

He sits down at Lydia's desk, and decides to go online to see what movies are playing. Better to placate her as much as possible.

At least at the movies she won't be blabbing her stupid head off at him.

As he clicks to connect to the web, a minimized page pops up from one of Lydia's AOL chats. It's a chat between Lydia and her brother Daniel from the night before.

Lydia: *How much oleander does it take to make a horse sick?*

Daniel: *Not much. A leaf or two will cause colic. Why? Your horse eat some?*

Lydia: *No. I need to get rid of some competition tomorrow. Scholarship.*

Daniel: *You're rotten. Be careful. It can kill the horse.*

Lydia: *I don't care.*

Daniel: *You are bad.*

Lydia: *I learned from the best. Gotta go. TTYL.*

"Bitch," Tristan says under his breath. He quickly presses print, then minimizes it again. Heart pounding, he yanks the paper off the printer and shoves it in his pocket just as Lydia comes out of the bathroom. "Were you printing something?"

"Uh, yeah, some movie options, but your printer didn't work."

"Oh. What looks good?"

"I don't know, let's look together while we walk down to my car. I'll guess we can look some up on my phone. My battery is a little low though."

"We can use mine," she chirps.

"Great. And what do you think about getting some ice cream at Cold Stone?"

"Ooh, yummy. That sounds even better."

For the first time in a long time, Tristan smiles and he means it. He's ecstatic. He will continue to fake it for one more night with Lydia. He has a plan brewing, and once he's worked out the details, he has a feeling he will no longer be under Lydia's thumb.

CHAPTER *forty-one*

The next day, Tristan sends Lydia a text telling her that he can't wait until the dance to see her, and for her to meet him at the Olympic House.

At first she teases him, telling him that he will just have to wait. And that she'll be worth it. He expects this from her and texts back that she will never forget the surprise he has for her, and that he really wants to give it to her now.

This hooks her.

She says that she'll commandeer one of academy's golf carts and be on her way.

He walks throughout the house, lighting candles. He's even gone so far as to place bouquets of roses in the room.

He waits. He checks his watch. It's four o'clock.

Twenty minutes later, Lydia shows up.

"Oh my God, Tristan," she says standing in the doorway. "This is beautiful. I thought, wow . . . I thought that maybe you didn't want to go through with it since, well, lately . . ." She walks over to him.

"I know I've been a little 'difficult,' but it's just because I love you so much and I want to be with you so badly. And this is amazing. But don't you want to wait until after the dance?"

"No. I don't."

She smiles, places her fingers on the top button of her blouse, and starts to unbutton it.

"No. Wait," he says.

She frowns at first, but then her eyes light up. "You want to undress me?"

"Remember that I said I had a surprise for you that you wouldn't forget?"

"Yes. It's beautiful what you've done here."

"Yeah. It is. But it isn't for you."

Her eyes narrow into hawk-like slits. "What?"

"It's not for you. All of this." He motions around the room. "It's actually for the person who should've won the event. It's for Vivienne. If she shows up."

"Are you kidding me? This isn't funny, Tristan!"

"Oh, I'm not trying to be funny, Lydia. It's just that paybacks are a bitch. Just like you."

She tosses her long blond hair back behind her shoulders and spins around, heading for the door. "You are so going to regret this! I am going to every media outlet, and the police, whoever will listen to me! Your father will be *ruined*, and so will you!"

"No, you're not going to do that," he states calmly.

"The hell I'm not!"

Tristan holds up a copy of her online chat. "I know what you did to Harmony. And I will tell . . . whatever it costs me."

"Excuse me?"

"I know that you're the one who caused Harmony to colic. Jesus, Lydia, you could have *killed* her!"

"I—I don't know what you're talking about."

He hands her the printout.

"This doesn't prove anything! You could have typed this up."

He shakes his head. "Yeah, but I didn't, and considering your IP address is on the printout, I think it's pretty clear that you wrote it."

She tears it up. "Now what?"

"I'm not stupid. I have a handful of others in a safe place, all of them in envelopes addressed to various people, including Holden, Kayla, Vivienne, and the police. What you did is a *crime*, Lydia."

She looks up at him, shaking with tears and anger. "What do you *want*, Tristan?"

"Not much, really. I want you to leave me alone. I am sick of you, and I am sick of your blackmail and your threats. If you go to anyone regarding my father, I will expose you and everyone will know who and what you are. And the thing is, with what you know about my family, I realize my father could go to prison. But I haven't done anything wrong. Plus, you'd have to prove he did those things. In your situation, at the very least, you will be kicked out of here, and the entire eventing community will know what you did. Not so sure that Christian Albright would want you on his team this summer when I tell him you poisoned a horse."

Tears are streaming down her face. It's the most real he's ever seen her look.

"I love you. I really love you."

"No, Lydia. You love the idea of perfect, and neither one of us is that. And I don't love you. So, do we have a deal? I live my life here, and you live yours? We stay out of each others' way, and we keep each others' secrets?"

"Deal," she finally hisses and heads to the door. As she is opening it, Vivienne is walking up the porch steps. She looks more than slightly stunned to see Lydia.

"I—I'm sorry," Vivienne says. "Riley is supposed to meet me here. We're working on our history project."

"Whatever, *Scholarship*. This one is all yours. Good luck."

Vivienne walks into the house, and looks at Tristan. "Looks like I interrupted something."

"No. You didn't interrupt anything. I want to talk to you."

"Okay, but Riley is supposed to meet me here at five."

"He isn't going to meet you. Come sit down over here with me, and I'll explain it all."

"Explain away. But I am standing right here."

"Okay, here goes. I talked to Riley, and he told me that you two aren't really going out. That you really are just friends. He told me about himself, about being gay, and that you knew."

"He did?"

"Yeah."

"Why would he tell *you* that?"

"Why? Because he knows I am totally insane over you."

She takes a step back, crosses her arms over her chest.

"Since the first day that I found you in Harmony's stall, I haven't stopped thinking about you, I kept asking Riley about you, I even dream about you. I just—God! I don't what else to say."

She doesn't respond for several agonizingly long seconds.

"What about Lydia? How can you be so *insane* over me, while planning your *big night*."

He knew this would come up, and he has thought it through. He hopes she will believe his explanation. Being partially truthful is his only option.

"See, I know how tough Lydia and her friends can make it, have made it, for you. I thought, maybe I could keep her in line, get her to leave you alone. And there really were several times when I got her to back off."

*Oh God, now she looks even more confused.*

"I, I guess I appreciate that. But uh … I'm sorry, but I'm still baffled here."

"I have already told you how I feel. I just need to know if you feel the same way. I see you look at me. I can feel something between us and from you—attraction, interest, and, okay, occasional disgust. Do I disgust you, Vivienne?"

A slow smile spreads across her face. "No."

"Good." When he takes her hand, she doesn't pull it away. "Lydia was here because I just broke up with her. I realize that you probably don't need a Prince Charming, or anyone to protect you. I also realize how stupid I've been to be with a girl that I can't stand. Especially when I'm crazy for someone else. For you." He looks into her eyes, trying desperately to read them. "I know I'm taking a chance here, but Vivienne, would you even consider just maybe, I don't know. Listen, Riley suggested this, or I wouldn't even bring it up, but would you go with me tomorrow night? Would you come with me to Homecoming?"

CHAPTER *forty-two*

I am stunned. There is no getting around that. I am fighting every emotion and feeling I have toward Tristan. This guy could mess up everything for me. How dare he be crazy insane for me, and tell me so, and send Lydia packing. I don't know if I should be pissed off, elated—all of that, or none of that. Damn.

When I walked up those steps to the Olympic House and saw Lydia and then Tristan, I felt sick to my stomach, sure they had just been together.

If I were some other girl, I might tell him that I feel the same way. That I'm crazy insane over him. That other than Harmony, he's all I think about.

But I don't.

I know what heartbreak looks like. I know what it feels like. And I know that humans break other humans' hearts. They just do.

So I say, "I promised Riley I would go with him." To my own ears, my voice sounds hard and metallic—emotionless.

He laughs nervously. "But it was Riley who insisted I tell you. He insisted I ask you to Homecoming. He understands. He does. You can ask him."

"Even so. I just don't think you and I would be . . . a good thing. We're not from the same world, and I have my goals, and they don't include a relationship."

"Vivienne, I totally respect your goals, and I would never get in the way of them."

"But you will. That will just happen."

"No. No. I swear it won't. I'm here to support you. I have the same dreams, you know. And sharing our dreams would make them even better." He reaches out and touches my cheek with his hand.

His hand is warm and strong; this thrumming rhythm starts to travel through my body. I've never had this kind of feeling before. His eyes, they are so intensely green, and I am seriously melting.

"Tell you what, Vivvie." He smiles, his finger against my lips. "Don't decide right now. Tomorrow night, if you show up, I'll know. If you don't, I'll know that. But maybe this will help your decision." Then he leans in and kisses my lips, ever so slowly, ever so sweetly. It's as if I am floating. And even as my brain is screaming, "Stop! Run!"—well, there are other parts of me that are shouting, "No way, sister! You stay right there because nothing has ever felt this good!"

I kiss him back. Both of his hands are on my face now, and I allow myself to float.

Mmm . . . delicious.

I have not forgotten Austen's kiss before I left for Fairmont. But as good as that was, it can't compete with the one Tristan has just given me.

His fingers skim the outlines of my cheekbone again, and he says, "Think on that." He stands and walks out, leaving me flushed and breathless.

CHAPTER *forty-three*

I am on some kind of cloud nine. Tristan waited outside for me, then drove me back from the Olympic House in one of the golf carts. We didn't say anything on the way back to campus. When we reached the barns, I asked him to drop me off so I could check on Harmony.

"I hope to see you tomorrow night," he said.

"We'll see," I tell him.

I go into Harmony's stall, happy to see how alert she is. She nuzzles me, and I wrap my arms around her. "Next time, big girl, no getting sick."

She shows me leaves again. "What are the leaves?" Then a picture emerges of a syringe of Banamine. "I know. It helped you." She sneezes, then she shows me a jar of bute.

"No, sweetie. We didn't give you any bute. You don't need any."

Now there's Serena's face. And then, for the first time, I hear Serena's voice. *They did this.*

"They? Who? What, Harmony?"

*They did this. They did this.*

My cell phone chimes with a new e-mail message. I take it from my pocket and see that the sender is sciencegirl18@gmail.com. The message in the subject line reads *Information you might want.*

Curious as any cat, I suck back a deep breath of air. Oh my God!

*You've received this ANONYMOUSLY. The file is in your tack trunk.*

The file? My tack trunk?


It has to be from Emily. But can information from her be trusted? What if this is just a stupid trick?

I call Riley and get his voice mail. "Hey, Ri, I think I might have some info on what happened to Dr. Miller. If you get this soon, I'm down in the tack room. I'll explain later."

Now, the big question: Do I look in the trunk?

I close Harmony's stall and make my way to the tack room. The barn aisle is dimly lit at this time of night, and I don't want to alert anyone to my presence by turning on the overhead lights. Once inside the tack room, I open my trunk.

Yep. Underneath my helmet bag is the file.

It is labeled *Haute Couture/Gallagher.* I close my trunk, sit on it, and begin reading.

I scan through a ten-page document that starts from when Dr. Miller was called out by Lydia to examine her horse. The report states that at that time, it appeared the horse was suffering from a minor colic. She was oiled, but not given any Banamine because she had a preexisting kidney condition. Lydia was given specific care instructions.

Dr. Miller saw the horse twice more that week before moving her to her hospital. Lydia requested that the horse be moved and treated at the equine hospital. The file noted that her parents were traveling overseas at the time on a cruise and could not be reached, but that her brother Daniel requested that the horse *not* be moved. But Kayla and Holden intervened and had the horse moved. Serena had taken excellent case notes.

How come Daniel had authority over the horses? And why he didn't want the mare taken to Serena's hospital? He didn't even give permission to treat the horse, although Holden, Kayla, and Lydia did.

The horse was treated at the hospital, and Serena wrote down a specific protocol. She took blood samples that were sent to a lab locally, as well as to a lab in Colorado.

Next page starts with this: "Cause of death: acute renal failure."

But what had caused Haute Couture's kidneys to fail?

When the horse was sent to Fairmont with Lydia, blood had been drawn. That was the protocol, according to Riley. Before new horses came onto the campus, they were first sent to Dr. Miller, who performed an extensive physical, including blood work.

The file states that when the mare came to the academy with Lydia, her blood work indicated that she had kidney sensitivity, but Dr. Miller put her on a protocol to manage the issue.

*Wait, what's this?* The file states that there was a "substantial" amount of bute and Banamine in Haute's system at the time of death. See, horses' kidneys are very efficient, but if someone doses a horse predisposed to kidney issues with a bute/Banamine combination over a period of time, the kidneys can get fried. And bute and Banamine are drugs any horse owner can easily get. There is a stock of both kept on hand at Fairmont—though it is kept under lock and key.

My gut is saying that someone poisoned Lydia's horse. Maybe even Lydia herself? Maybe her brother, Daniel? Or Christian Albright? Holden? And Emily must believe that someone intentionally murdered the mare, or she wouldn't have left the file for me, right?

Could Lydia have done something this heinous? If so, why? Did Serena Miller figure it all out, and was she killed because of that?

There is something way bigger here. Yes, you can go to jail for killing an animal. But if you murder a person over it, you'd risk going to prison for the rest of your life.

What kind of person would be willing to take that risk? Have I—have we—all been walking around with a killer among us?

I think of all of the cop shows I've watched over the years, and some of the thrillers I've read. Love and money causes people to murder. So do secrets. And revenge.

But I couldn't help thinking that all of this led back to Haute Couture—a horse worth a lot of money. The Banamine/bute would not have caused many vets to think much about it. Many of them would have thought that the horse was colicking when she was really going into renal failure. With what looks like colic, blood isn't always taken, but a certain protocol is followed, and that typically includes dosing with Banamine to relieve the initial discomfort.

Maybe it was the bute that came into question—why the combination?—but a savvy owner would know how to handle it. The thing was that Serena had been caring for this horse for the two years that Lydia was at Fairmont. She knew about the animal's kidney problems. Same with Lydia.

No necropsy had been ordered because it was accepted that this horse had died from a preexisting condition.

But, from what is in this file, it is clear that Serena had her doubts. Had she drawn blood at the time she euthanized the horse, suspicious that something else had occurred? Had something, or someone, tipped her off? Or was she just being extra cautious? Serena could have also taken hair from the horse's mane or tail and had those sent into a lab.

Someone had poisoned Lydia's horse. Serena figured it out and knew who it was. She likely planned to do a few things. Things I would have done. First, I would have called the USEA, USET, and the company that had insured the horse, because if I had to put a motive on it, it was all about money.

*Money and greed and murder.* I lean back against the wall of the tack room, wondering just how much Haute Couture was insured for, and who owned the insurance policy. It couldn't be anyone under eighteen—like Lydia. And her parents, they had to have oodles of cash. But what if Daniel . . .

CHAPTER *forty-four*

I go back into Harmony's stall. When I place my hands on either side of her neck, she nuzzles me. "Hi, you. I am getting closer. There are answers here." I hold up the file to her.

Harmony shifts her weight from the back right to the left, then pricks her ears forward.

"What is it?" My hand slides down her face, and she moves away. I am feeling fear from her, and then she shows me the baseball cap again. "I know. I know whoever did this, he had the cap on. Maybe the jacket. Was it Holden?" I can't—or just don't want to—believe that Holden did this.

Harmony snorts. She is agitated. No, it's more than that. She is afraid.

As I am setting the file back in the trunk, Harmony lets out a shrill whinny.

I whirl around to see what the problem is and am stopped short.

Standing in the doorway is Newman Becker—wearing a baseball cap and a Fairmont jacket. "Newman?"

He is pulling a gun from his jacket pocket. "Sorry, kid, but you should have minded your own business." He glances from side to side. "I'll take that file. My truck is right behind the barn. You're going to come with me. And you are going to do it quietly."

*Cannot move. Cannot think.*

"C'mon, Vivienne, I am not joking here."

"Wh-what if I w-won't go with you?"

"Well then, here is the deal, Vivienne: if you don't go with me, I'll have to do something really awful, and I'll be able to make your little boyfriend Riley take the blame. You won't believe the stories I can come up with. It won't be too hard to make it sound like Riley had a major jealousy issue over how great a rider you are."

"What are you talking about?" I stammer.

"I wired Harmony's stall with explosives, and if you don't do what I tell you, all I have to do is push a button." He takes out some kind of remote from his jacket. "Harmony, Sebastian, and maybe even a few others will never make it out alive."

"N-no one will believe you."

"Oh, I think they will. And I am completely willing to take that chance. Now, you, me, and Emily are going to take a ride in my truck."

"Oh my God. Emily."

"Oh, yes, I've taken care of her. So if you want to make sure these horses live and Riley continues his cushy life, then you will come with me, nice and quietly."

Dizzy-swirly-colors-in-the-brain are happening. What has he

228  MICHELE SCOTT

done with Emily? How did he find out where I was? I can hear Harmony pawing the ground in her stall.

Newman shoves the gun in my side, and we walk out of the tack room together. I am trying not to pee my pants, and Harmony is whinnying in distress.

He unlocks the truck and shoves me in the passenger seat. I see Emily on the floor of the backseat, bound and gagged. Her eyes are red-rimmed and wild with fear.

*What can I do? Can I help her? Is he going to do that to me, too?*

Newman turns the key in the ignition, and we begin pulling out slowly.

"What do you plan to do?" I ask.

He doesn't answer at first. "You sure are a curious young woman. I've been watching you and Emily. Overheard your little chat the other day in the tack room. I started thinking that I needed to take care of this issue. I hoped Emily was smarter than to clue you in. I was wrong."

"Can I just ask you why?"

"Why what?"

"Why did you kill Lydia Gallagher's horse, and then murder Dr. Miller? And how did you even figure out I was onto the truth?"

"It wasn't just me. Why do you think?"

"For the insurance money?"

"She was insured for half a million. But I figured she had some issues that would keep her from ever being the very best, so in a way I actually did her a service."

"But you're a famous guy. And it's not like you're poor."

"Ah, you want a better reason. Yeah, well, let's just say I could see problems down the road for this horse. Let's just say that Lydia's big brother was once a student of mine, and that Daniel Gallagher knew I've had some recent financial issues. So I told him about the mare, he told me what she was insured for, and we made a deal. If I got rid of the horse, he'd give me half of the insurance money, plus I'd help Lydia find a new horse and would make a commission from the sale. Win-win-win. See, poor little rich girl's mom and dad have no real interest in her or her horses. Daniel, on the other hand, likes to runs things, and he knows when it is a good idea to scratch the back of someone who has helped him in the past.

"As for how I found out about you being a little snoop? You shouldn't have upset Lydia by asking questions about her dead horse. She tells Daniel everything. He gave me a call, let me know that you might cause us a problem. I spotted Emily leaving the tack room the other night, and saw you follow her out. That gave me reason to keep an eye on her. I actually set you up with that text from Emily's phone about the file. She gave it up to me. Not like she had a choice. And, before you ask, Lydia has no idea. None. She'd never be able to handle something like this. Not yet, anyway."

"But why kill Dr. Miller?"

He held up a hand, and I could see the shiny metal of the gun from the moonlight coming in the window.

"Okay, that wasn't supposed to happen that way. Serena called me and said she suspected I had doped the horse over time in order to get the commission on the new horse. She hadn't put the insurance thing together yet, but I didn't want to take the chance. I went to talk with her that night. She was in her barn, on the ladder, and she told me she planned to report me to Kayla, Holden, the USEA,

FEI, USET, and anyone else she thought needed to know. And I got a little angry. But all I did was give that damn ladder a little shake. How was I supposed to know she'd come down like that and hit her head?"

"You could have called for help!"

He clucks his tongue and shakes his head. "She was basically dead when she hit the ground, kid. Just a piece of bad luck for her. But it was a way out of the whole thing for me—until you came along. And now it's my turn to ask: How in the hell did you get a whiff of this stuff?"

"Let's just say I had some inside information."

"From Emily?"

"No. An entirely different source."

"Dammit. You have talent. I never in a million years would have thought that either one of you would put me in this position."

We are pulling out of the long drive that leads up to Fairmont, which means we will soon be turning out onto Highway 101.

Just as he makes the turn out onto the highway, something catches my eye in the back of the truck. Wait a minute. Not something.

It's someone.

# RILEY

## CHAPTER *forty-five*

R iley was working out when Vivvie left him the message about going to the tack room.

By the time he made it down to the barn, Newman was next to her, walking out the back way. The gun shocked him to his core. He didn't know what to do. His heart was racing. He had to help. But how?

As Newman forced her into the truck, Riley climbed into the back.

Now they are exiting the drive, nearing the entrance to the highway. Riley is lying flat on the bed of the truck, not moving. He sends a text to Kayla Fairmont. *In big trouble. Stop Newman's truck. Has Vivienne and Emily. Has a gun! Heading south 101.*

A minute later his phone vibrates. It's Kayla, but how can he dare answer? He sends another text. *Am in the bed of the truck. Help!*

Now what should he do?

Then he hears them. Sirens.

They are growing closer.

And Newman begins driving faster.

As the truck rounds a corner on the Pacific Coast Highway, Riley is hurtled against the side of the truck, hard.

He knows the beach is to the right of them and that they are heading into Malibu. Though there are sinister twists all along this stretch of the highway, Newman keeps up the speed.

*Rounding a bend, truck spinning out of control, plunging off the side of the highway.*

And Riley is thrown from the bed.

CHAPTER *forty-six*

I am with Dean. We are on a trail ride through the Cascades. The scent of the tall pine trees is clean and divine. The sky above is a cloudless blue, and rays from the sun beat down gently on our backs. A hawk flies overhead as we cross a flowing stream. All is perfect. All is quiet. All is serene.

And then—

Sounds of alarms screeching through my ears. I see so many faces. Faces I don't recognize.

"Pressure is dropping, Doctor!"

*Doctor?*

More shouting and beeps, and then *I am back in the Cascades with Dean. We reach the edge of a forest and it opens up into a meadow.*

*A horse is coming toward us. Harmony.*

*We ride up to her, and in his way Dean tells me to go and ride her. I get off his back and climb onto hers.*

*Harmony takes me out past the meadow and down to a field—a cross-country course is set up, and we are cantering and jumping the obstacles, clearing them easily.*

I wake up to the sound of my own harsh breathing.

It hurts so much to breathe. But my mother's face is looking down at me.

"Mom?"

"*Shhh. Shnoopy. Shhh.*"

"Mom?"

"It's okay, sweetie, you are okay."

I am in a hospital. The last thing I remember is the truck flying over the side of the highway. *Oh God, Emily. And Riley.* "My friends?"

Mom takes my hand. "They are a little beaten up, just like you are. You actually got the worst of it."

"When did you get here?" I whisper. "How long have I been here?"

"You were unconscious for a little while, Viv. And they had to put some pins in your ankle. But it's a miracle that you are all really okay. I got here about an hour ago."

"Pins?"

She nods.

"When can I ride again?"

She kind of laughs and cries at the same time. "That's my girl."

"No, I mean it, Mom. When can I ride again?"

"Doctor says probably at least two months."

"Mom, can I stay at Fairmont? Can I stay with Harmony?"

"I'll have to think about that."

"Please, Mom?"

"Okay, Viv. Yes. You can."

"Becker? What happened to Newman Becker?"

"He's in jail."

"Good."

A wave of fatigue begins to take over. "What time is it, Mom?"

"About three in the morning, Shnoopy. Go back to sleep."

I do just that.

When I wake the next day, I am really sore. But my mom is still here. Flowers fill the room.

Kayla and Holden, and Martina and her parents, come to see me.

Holden tells us that Newman told the police the same story he had told me, and that Daniel Gallagher is now also in jail. Kayla says that Lydia is devastated and feels horrible about what has happened to Emily, Riley, and me.

That night my mom and I are watching TV when she stands up and says, "Hey, Viv, I think I'm going to go down to the cafeteria and grab a bite. You okay?"

"Yes, Mom. I am. Go eat." We have just learned that they are letting me out of this place tomorrow.

About five minutes after Mom leaves, Riley, Martina, and Emily show up. "Hey!"

I get hugs from Riley and Martina. Emily manages a smile. I'll take a smile, for now. "No Homecoming for you three?"

"We can have our own dance party," Martina says.

Riley kisses my cheek. "We have a surprise for you," he says.

Martina holds up her iPod, and a few seconds later Taylor Swift singing "I'm Only Me When I Am with You" queues up. As I'm laughing, Emily says, "But you can't have Homecoming without a guy in a tux."

"What?" I say.

Tristan walks in, tux and all, with a bouquet of roses. Oh my God, I am wearing a gross hospital gown. What do I look like?

"What are you guys doing?" I ask.

"Night, Vivvie," says Riley.

"Martina? Emily?" I plead.

Martina sets the iPod down, and my friends leave the room.

Tristan sits on the edge of my bed. "You scared me, Vivienne Taylor."

"Sorry," I mutter.

He hands me a card. "Open it."

It's a get-well card showing a horse with an old-school ice bag on his head. I open it, and two tickets fall out.

"A little birdie told me that you like Taylor Swift, and since she's coming to town, I was wondering if you'd go with me. As friends, of course. I know you have your goals and all."

I roll my eyes at him and reach up, grabbing his coat lapel. Even though I'm sore and hurt, I pull Tristan in to me and we share another one of those amazing, delicious best kisses in the world.

"Friends? You know what? We are so going to this concert as more than just friends," I say once we finish with that amazing, delicious kiss.

"I was hoping you'd say that."

"Yeah. Well, I just did."

Then Tristan Goode kisses me again.

When I get out of the hospital, I'll let Harmony know that the bad man is gone. And maybe I'll find out if anything is going on between Kayla and Christian. Or get Emily to tell me more about what happened to Haute Couture. And I am also concerned about the growing threat that seems to surround Martina and her family. And Riley, he has a long road ahead of him, and will need a good friend to help him navigate that road.

God, I am even concerned about how Lydia Gallagher is going to react to all of this. Maybe I'll get it all figured out. Maybe I won't.

But for now, in Tristan's arms and lost in his kisses, all of those questions, all of those worries . . . well, I am going to set them all aside, and just live.

In this moment.

# ACKNOWLEDGMENTS

Things always happen for a reason and in their own time. This book/series is a perfect example of that. The character of Vivienne Taylor and her unique gift with horses has been in the back of my mind for years. I have to acknowledge those very special people who gave me the freedom and green light to write this book exactly the way that I wanted to.

First off, is my dearest friend Jessica Park. I couldn't ask for a better support system and friend. She's seen me through the good, the bad, and the ugly. And, without her making the introduction between Timothy Ditlow and me, this series would still be in the back of my mind. Thank You, JP, for opening the door and insisting I pitch the series.

Thank You, Tim, for believing in Vivvie as much as I do, and for taking a chance on this. As we said that night at Rick Bayless' amazing restaurant that this was meant to be. Who would have ever known that the evening before you were at a dressage barn? Also, thanks again for that dinner. It's one I will never forget.

Thanks to my agent Scott Miller of Trident Media. It is truly wonderful when an author feels like her agent has her back, and will go the extra mile for her. Scott does this with every project, and I am grateful to have him on board.

Huge props and gratitude to my very good friend Gina Miles. I can't even express how truly appreciative I am for your friendship, your support, and your guidance. You are an amazing woman.

Same goes to Terri Rocovich—always there for me, my horses, and my family. I am blessed to have such wonderful horse women in my life!

Amy Hosford is another person who deserves a thank you from me. Your help in getting this book to print means a lot. As well as the entire team at ACP, especially the cover artists!

It may sound crazy to thank a horse because she can't read this, but I want to acknowledge her anyway. My mare Krissy has been one of the kindest animals I've had the privilege to own. She's in her final days now, but she has taught me a lot about myself, others, and how to be graceful under pressure. I can't do it like she does, but I'll keep trying. In many ways, Krissy is the horse who inspired Harmony's character. She will always hold a special place in my heart.

Finally, thank you to the eventing community at large. Eventers and their horses are courageous, gorgeous, and simply put--competing in the best sport there is.

# Michele Scott lives in California

with her family. With her days spent in the barn or at the keyboard, Ms. Scott has forged a flourishing career as mystery writer and is also deeply involved in the world of horses and equestrian riding.